Bridging the Heart

Kindred Spirits Mysteries

Beth Connor

Wolf Grove Media, LLC

Copyright © 2024 by Beth Connor

All rights reserved.

No portion of this book may be reproduced in any form without written permission from the publisher or author, except as permitted by U.S. copyright law.

Contents

CHAPTER ONE

Whispers from the Past

C lara froze, the sound of laughter and whispers slicing the silence. There, Ethan was entwined with another woman, her face now burned into Clara's memory, shattering all trust.

Without a word, she turned, fleeing into the rain-drenched streets of Boston. Her heart pounded a frantic rhythm that matched her steps. She found herself poised at the threshold of a decision. Before her loomed a neon-lit entrance of a bar, its raucous laughter and the clink of glasses tempting her into oblivion. Yet something within her recoiled. She felt a silent plea for solitude over the solace found in the bottom of a glass. With a breath, she turned her back on the bar and made her way to the sanctuary that promised a different refuge—the Boston Public Library.

As she approached, its grandeur stood stark against the darkening sky. It was a beacon for lost souls seeking respite. Clara stepped into the embrace of the library, leaving behind the chaos that had torn through her existence only hours before. The image was a vision that scorched her insides, amplified because the apartment was *hers*—every bill had her name on it.

Inside the library, Clara wandered the endless shelves, but it was in the periodicals section she found her true escape. A magazine on New England Hauntings caught her eye, its pages whispering of mysteries and echoes from the past. In particular, the story of Anne of the Willows captivated her. It was as if Anne's tale mirrored her own—a story of love lost and betrayal that resonated with her soul.

She looked around to ensure she was alone, then did something she had never considered before. With a mix of desperation and defiance, she tore the page from the magazine. This act of rebellion was unlike Clara, yet the story of Anne of the Willows was a light in her storm, a connection she did not want to leave behind.

When she exited the library, the city of Boston lay transformed by the rain into a reflective maze. Back home, the apartment was silent. The woman and Ethan had gone, leaving behind only the faint trace of unfamiliar perfume and a careless note. Clara, with the torn page from the magazine clutched in her hand, stood amidst the remnants of her previous life and picked up the note.

The rain tapped on the window, each droplet a punctuation of the words that Clara couldn't seem to tear her gaze from. As the dim lighting of her apartment cast long shadows, emphasizing her solitude, Clara found herself surrounded by mementos of happier times — the ashtray she stole during their first vacation together, now holding the dying remnants of a burnt-out candle, and photos of shared laughs, kisses, and moments strewn across the coffee table.

The worn, blue rug beneath her feet, where they'd collapsed in giggles one evening, now felt cold and detached, much like the words from his letter and the echoing silence of the apartment. With each paragraph read and reread, the sorrow of her own story mingled with the intrigue of another's—Anne of the Willows. This would be her next novel, and with it she would rise like a phoenix.

Clara's heart ached for Anne. The tale of a woman waiting by the willow-lined bank for a lover who never came sparked a flame within Clara. It was a mystery wrapped in the soft veil of the past, yet it felt as urgent.

Drawing a deep breath, she set the letter aside, letting the pain it brought recede into the shadows. Her focus shifted, eyes landing her laptop. Clara felt a stir of excitement, a pull towards something beyond the confines of her sorrow. Here was a story that needed telling, a mystery that called to her with its silent whispers and unanswered questions.

Determined, Clara powered on the computer, the soft hum cutting through the rain's incessant patter. As Clara tapped the keys, she outlined Anne's story with her own, drawing closer to the mysteries shrouded around Willows Bridge. Yet, even as she delved into the realm of intrigue, her focus was hijacked by the biting contents of the letter lying beside her.

Taking a deep breath, she paused and gripped at the single sheet of paper. An affair laid bare. A conclusion without closure. Hollow apologies that resonated with the emptiness within her. The sharp sting of betrayal blurred her surroundings, pooling tears in her eyes. She pondered on the ruin that love had become.

They had charged the atmosphere in the room with electricity just weeks prior. The air had been thick with vanilla from the candles, the warm aroma intertwined with their breaths, creating a heady mix of sensation and emotion. As a sultry song played in the background, her fingers had grazed his cheek, pulling him close. They had been lost in heartbeats and rustling fabric, synchronized. Everything had felt so right, so perfect. Now, as Clara's gaze refocused on the present, the cruel irony was not lost on her. That deep connection, that undeniable passion, was gone.

The air in the room pressed down, making each breath a struggle. Clara's fingertips tightened around the edges of the paper, crumpling it. Her eyes darted over the words once more, each sentence, each confession, plunging her deeper into a whirlpool of emotions. A bitter taste formed in the back of her throat. Every "I love you," every stolen kiss, every promise—it all felt like a cruel mockery now.

She felt her heartbeat racing and a surge of anger boiling up inside. "How could he do this? Throw everything away?" she thought, glaring at the letter in her hand. It seemed to her that he was using those inked words as a shield, dodging the confrontation. She stood, the need to escape the moment pressing upon her. The letter slipped from her grasp, fluttering to the floor like a wounded bird.

"It's not you, it's me," she said, mimicking his words. The phrase seemed so trite, so insincere. A clichéd excuse for a clichéd betrayal.

She paused at the window, staring out at the city lights. The energy of the city, so full of promise and adventure, now felt alien. The shadows of the night echoed her own darkness, and the city's heartbeat felt out of sync.

As the reality of the situation sank in, her anger waned, giving way to an overwhelming sadness.

"Why?" The question, raw and heavy, hung in the air, unanswered.

Without thinking, she found herself in the kitchen, glass in hand. Pouring herself a drink. The old Clara would've let herself be consumed by the comfort the drink promised, especially when thinking of those nights with Ethan and their hot and cold relationship, the highs of love and music, the lows of fights and substances. But as she raised the glass to her lips, she felt the weight of the coin she carried in her pocket.

She remembered her journey to sobriety, her battles, her determination, and the promises she had made to herself. She thought of the times she had resisted, of the support she had gained, of the hope she held onto.

With an exhale, she moved to the window, looking out at the streets of Boston. She tilted the glass, letting the wine spill out, each drop symbolizing the choices she had made and the ones she was yet to make. As the wine pooled on the windowsill, the familiar sound of a key jingling sounded at the door.

Before she could process, the door creaked, revealing Ethan in all his glory. He pushed it open, looking as though he'd walked through a storm, perhaps expecting a tempest within as well. And he wasn't wrong. Without hesitation, she threw the letter at him, her voice raised in a torrent of emotion. "You couldn't even face me? A damn letter, really?!"

He winced, surprised by the storm in Clara's eyes. "Clara, I... I'm sorry."

"Sorry?" Her voice crackled with scorn, inches from his face. "You think a letter makes this easier?"

"I didn't know how else to say it," he confessed.

"So, you drop this bombshell in a letter? Coward," she spat, the letter crinkling in her clenched fist.

The air between them was electric, charged with a history too deep to sever. He reached out, a reflex from a time now past, but she stood her ground, her resolve a barrier between them.

"It was a mistake. Please, can we just forget about the letter, and..." Ethan's voice trailed off, the name of the other woman lingering unspoken between them.

"Forget?" Clara's voice was icy. "How can I forget?"

He looked at her, desperation etched across his face. "Wasn't it real? Everything we had?"

"It was real, too real. But it's over," she replied.

"So, that's it? You're just giving up on us?" Ethan narrowed his eyes.

"It's not giving up. It's moving forward. This," she waved the letter, "is about you figuring out who you are without me."

Ethan's stance stiffened, defiance flickering in his eyes. "I can't just walk away. We can't throw everything we had over a mistake. I know I can make things right."

Clara's gaze was unwavering. He wasn't lost without her, he was lost without her money. "A mistake? Ethan, your 'mistake' broke us. You decided it was over the moment you wrote this letter." She paused, the anger simmering in her veins. "And now you want to pretend it never happened?"

He took a step closer, desperation edging his voice. "Isn't what we had worth fighting for? I'm not giving up that easily."

"Fighting for? You chose this." Clara's hand dove into her purse, pulling out a handful of cash. With a swift movement, she flung it at him. "Here, for a hotel tonight. I'll be gone in the morning. And Ethan," her voice was cold, "you have one month to get your things out, then I'm changing the locks."

The money hit him with a soft thud, falling to the ground. Ethan's face was a mask of conflict.

"Clara, please—" he started, but the finality in her stance told him there was no room for negotiation.

"Goodbye, Ethan."

Ethan picked up the scattered bills. She watched him, the emptiness already settling in. He walked to the door, pausing, before stepping out into the night, leaving her alone in the aftermath.

These feelings weren't new to Clara. They were all too familiar.

She sat in the ruins of another failed relationship. Memories of her parents surged to the forefront. She remembered the whispered arguments late at night, the slammed doors, the icy silences that could stretch for days. Her mother's eyes, often red-rimmed and distant, her father's stoic face as he tried to pretend everything was alright.

The pain her mother felt, the cycle of hope and heartbreak, seemed to have imprinted on Clara. She'd promised herself she wouldn't end up like her mother, entrapped in a cycle of loving, trusting, and then getting hurt. And yet, here she was, feeling like history was playing a cruel joke, repeating itself with her at the center.

Clara hugged her knees, trying to find solace in her own embrace. She'd broken her own vow, become another casualty in the cyclical pattern of heartbreak that seemed to be her family's legacy.

After clearing the coffee table, she moved her laptop with a purpose in mind: to find a retreat. The story of Anne of the Willows was set in Stowe, Vermont—a location not even a half-day's drive away. Determined, she planned to get a place for the month, a sanctuary away from her heartache, where she could focus on her novel.

The allure of the little town, with its majestic mountains, rolling landscapes, and serene forests, captivated her. Anne's tale, mirroring Clara's own turbulent emotions, felt fitting. She saw Stowe's beauty as the perfect muse for her writing.

Without delay, Clara browsed for accommodations. She stumbled upon a listing for a cabin tucked away in the woods less then a half mile away from the bridge. The images revealed a warm, inviting interior with a stone fireplace, enveloped by towering trees. It seemed destined. With a few decisive clicks, she booked the place from May 14th to June 14th, hopeful that the coming month would offer the peace and clarity she sought.

The journey to Stowe was as much a voyage through Clara's inner self as it was through the hills and valleys of Vermont. As the car's tires hummed on the asphalt, Clara's mind played a slideshow of recent events, interspersed with fragments of memories both cherished and painful.

With every mile she covered, the city's cacophony grew fainter, replaced by the symphony of nature. Mountains stood tall, their peaks caressed by the early morning mist, while dense forests flanked the road, their canopies creating a serene green tunnel. The mirror-like lakes reflected the azure sky, offering her moments of tranquility and reflection.

As Clara's car meandered through the quaint towns and picturesque landscapes, she'd occasionally tune into local radio stations to break the solitude. Amid the casual chatter and local news, a segment on Vermont legends piqued her interest. The voice of the radio host introduced a series of local myths, but one stood out, echoing with resonance in her own life.

"... and of course, who can forget the haunting tale of Anne of the Willows? Legend has it that a young woman named Anne, heartbroken and betrayed by her lover, took her own life on that very bridge," the radio host began. The story was told in a somber tone, painting a vivid picture of a love that promised forever, only to shatter in the cruel hands of fate.

It was clear this story was following her. As Clara listened, every word seemed to strike a chord deep within. She could feel Anne's pain, her despair, the crushing weight of betrayal. The familiarity of it all was unsettling, yet comforting. It was as if the spirit spoke to anyone who's known heartbreak.

Clara was enthralled by the complex emotions and the dance between history and today, affection and sorrow. This concept blossomed into more than mere preoccupation—it was becoming a means for Clara to navigate and comprehend her experiences. She realized Anne's tale embodied the essence of love's resilience and its fragilities. Visiting the actual location propelled her to enrich the story further. There was an inexplicable pull, a magnetism that was hard to ignore.

The cabin Clara had rented was everything she had envisioned—a peaceful retreat, miles away from the chaotic remnants of her life. The sun hung low in the sky, casting its light over the landscape, painting the lush Vermont scenery with a touch of amber brilliance.

And then there was Willows Bridge.

Clara found herself drawn to it right away. The blend of heartache and mystery intertwined with her own emotions, compelling her to seek its roots firsthand. This wasn't just research—it was a personal quest, inviting her to step into the heart of the tale.

As she approached, the bridge seemed to materialize out of the fading daylight. The ancient wood, darkened by age and weather, created a backdrop against the evening sky. It was a structure frozen in time, its legacy written in every grain and groove. The setting sun made the shadows dance upon its wooden panels, making it appear the bridge breathed with memories of the past.

After parking her car at a distance, Clara walked the remaining stretch. With every step she took, a distinct chill crept over her. It was almost summer, and the evening was warm, but the cold she felt was deep, almost bone-chilling. The bridge seemed to exude an energy of its own.

The soft gurgle of the water beneath was like a muted lullaby, a counterpoint to the eerie ambiance. But as she ventured further onto the bridge, another sound emerged. The creaking of wood was expected, but the faint whispers that danced around her were not. These weren't the murmurs of visitors or the rustling of trees; they were something else, distant yet present. It was as if the very air around her was charged with the lingering echoes of Anne's lament.

She hugged her arms around herself, goosebumps prickling her skin. Clara tried to shake off the growing sense of unease. And just when she thought she might've imagined it all, out of the corner of her eye, she saw her.

A fleeting vision of a young woman, pale and ethereal, her silhouette undiscernible in the dimming light. Her dress, though spectral, bore the marks of another era, and her face seemed etched with sorrow. But as quickly as the apparition appeared, it vanished, leaving Clara to question if it had been real.

She tried to make sense of the scene before her. The tales that had been distant, mere stories she had read or heard on the radio that she had forced into her own narrative. Yet, standing on the bridge now, they took on an undeniable reality.

With a shaky breath, Clara decided it was enough for one evening. The bridge, with its stories and spirits, would be there tomorrow. For now, she needed the solace of her cozy cabin, a warm cup of tea, and perhaps the comforting pages of her journal to make sense of the overwhelming emotions of the day.

The next morning, the sun filtered through the windows of Maple's Brew, a small cafe that seemed to be a hub for the locals in Stowe. The aroma of fresh pastries and roasted coffee lured Clara in from her morning walk. She chose a table by the window, hoping to find inspiration in the peaceful morning scenes of the town.

As she waited for her order, muted conversations filled the cafe, creating a comfortable background hum. As she was lost in her thoughts, a voice broke through.

"You're not from around here, are you?" a voice, seasoned with age, broke her reverie. She looked up to see an elderly man, with snowy hair and a face mapped with wrinkles.

"Just arrived yesterday. It's quite beautiful," Clara responded.

"Ah, drawn by the tales, then?" He nodded towards her journal on the table, while cradling Clara's last novel in his other hand, her portrait on the back cover smiling back at them.

Clara paused, her hand suspended in the air, clutching her coffee. "Yes, actually," she said, breaking into a smile and gesturing for him to join her.

The old man took the seat across from her and leaned in, a move Clara matched, captivated by his energy.

He began, "There's a legend, dear, woven into the fabric of this town. The tale of Anne of the Willows." His voice dipped, a solemn prelude. Clara chuckled. "I've heard bits and pieces," she confessed, eager not to overshadow his version of the story. Her mind wandered back to the encounter from the night before. The elderly man nodded, his voice taking on a reverent tone. "It's a sad story. A young woman, full of life and love, betrayed by the one she trusted most. Left waiting on that bridge for a lover who never came. And when her heart couldn't bear that pain, she took her own life, hanging from the very rafters of the bridge she'd hoped would be the start of her new life."

The cafe seemed to grow quieter, other conversations dimming as if out of respect for the tragic tale. Anne's pain and anguish echoed her own heartbreak, the sting of betrayal still raw.

He continued, "It's said her spirit still lingers, trapped between worlds. Many have seen her, especially on those misty evenings. She waits, hoping that maybe, just maybe, her lover will return." The tale continued. Anne's story, a poignant echo of Clara's recent wounds, left her with a lump in her throat.

"Thank you," Clara said.

The man nodded and held out the novel, her novel, Clara's face gazing up from the back cover. "Would you?" he asked, sliding the book towards her with a hopeful expectancy.

From one storyteller to another, Clara inscribed, her hand steady but her heart tumultuous.

With a sense of purpose, Clara thanked the man, leaving the cafe with more than just the taste of coffee on her lips. It was still strange when people recognized her. Success had come hard and fast. But now, the tragedy of Anne, and her own heartbreak was waiting to be penned.

That evening, Clara returned to the bridge, her heart aflutter with unease. Its wooden frame a portal to the past, stood bathed in the glow of twilight. Shadows nestled in its crevices, the structure arching over the murmuring river below. The lantern in her hand cast a light that battled the encroaching darkness, its light reflecting off the varnished wood and creating an eerie atmosphere. The silence was punctuated only by the distant call of an owl and the gentle whisper of the river.

Settling near the center, Clara placed her notebook on her lap, the light next to her provided just enough illumination to jot down her thoughts.□

She wrote of love's ghosts, the echoes of those lost, their

presence felt but unseen. "Love, when lost, leaves behind ghosts that never fade," she penned. A chilling gust swept across the bridge. Startled, Clara gripped her notebook, but the wind whipped the loose pages free, sending them dancing into the darkness. She watched, helpless, as her words vanished.

The bridge seemed to sigh, the air thick with tales of love and betrayal. Then, she saw her—a figure at the bridge's end, a wisp of history and heartache, her presence a fleeting glimpse into a bygone era.

Heart pounding, Clara was transfixed. The ghostly figure and she shared a moment of silent communion, an exchange of understanding.

A soft whisper floated through the air, so faint that Clara strained to catch it. Words of love, promises made, and dreams shattered echoed around her, tales of timeless betrayal that tugged at her very soul. "Wait for me," the voice pleaded, carrying with it centuries of hope and anguish.

The vision faded, but the presence lingered. Clara took a shaky breath, collecting her scattered thoughts and pages. What she'd witnessed was both haunting and heart-wrenching. Anne's spirit, still tethered to this world by the chains of her tragic past, sought solace, understanding, and perhaps, a voice. Still shaking, Clara wondered if it would be better to visit the bridge tommorow, in the d aylight.

Nestled in the cabin, Clara leaned against the headboard, her legs cocooned in a quilt, with her notebook balanced on her legs. The faint chorus of crickets from outside softened the profound stillness that enveloped the room.

She wrote, letting the ink flow, guided by the raw emotions from the day's experiences. "Loneliness," she began, "isn't just the absence. It's the void left by their memories, the silent spaces that once echoed with laughter and whispered secrets." She felt those words, the pain of abandonment, the sting of betrayal—emotions she now shared with Anne.

Her hand faltered as memories rushed back. She could almost feel Ethan's warm hands and the shared moments of quiet affection. But interwoven with these recollections were the seeds of doubt, the overlooked signs, and the ultimate revelation of betrayal that had shattered everything. The line between joy and sorrow had become indistinct, each memory tainted by the knowledge of what was to come.

Drained from the rush of emotions, Clara set aside her notebook and lay down, pulling the quilt over her. The distant howl of the wind ushered her into a restless sleep.

In her dream, Clara was transported back to her old apartment, nestled in Ethan's embrace. As the comfort of their shared moments enveloped her, the scene shifted—the softness beneath her transformed into the unyielding expanse of Willows Bridge. In the distance, Anne's figure emerged.

As the dream unfolded, Anne's presence grew more menacing. With a sudden surge of anger, the ghostly apparition lunged towards Ethan, jolting Clara awake.

Clara, drenched in sweat and with her heart racing, grappled with the imagery of her nightmare. Anne's transformation from a passive figure to a wrathful ghost in her dream mirrored the unresolved anger and hurt that lingered within, painting a haunting picture.

CHAPTER TWO

The Engineer and the Novelist

A symphony of bird calls serenaded Clara on her morning walk toward Willows Bridge. The trail wound itself through the woods, and she breathed in the earthy perfume of pine and spruce. Dapples of sunlight played across the path, casting a magic that lifted her imagination into flight. She half-expected to glimpse a fairy, perhaps perched on a fern or on a rabbit's back. This place was full of magical tales with each tree and shadow a piece of the enchantment.

About a half mile into her walk, the dense curtain of foliage parted to unveil her destination. Yet, as she approached, it wasn't the bridge that captured her attention, but a figure. The man was engrossed in his task. Every gesture he made was a intriguing. Clara couldn't help but wonder if there was more to him than met the eye—perhaps a touch of the fey, a guardian of secrets old as the bridge itself.

Curiosity piqued, Clara took a few steps closer. The gentle crunch of gravel beneath her shoes marked her approach. She angled herself, attempting to get a glimpse over his shoulder. Her eyes traced the sweeping lines of his sketches and the meticulous notes he'd penned down. The drawings showcased the bridge's architecture, but there was an artistic flair to them, showing a deep appreciation of its beauty.

The light filtering through the trees illuminated his features. There he stood, a vision of confidence with a sprinkle of vulnerability that Clara found irresistible. She couldn't help but laugh at herself. Here she was again, painting strangers with the colors of her imagination, much like she had once colored Ethan in hues of unwarranted virtues. That ordeal had taught her a lesson—or so she thought. Ethan had been anything but the romantic hero she'd imagined him to be.

Determined not to repeat history, Clara had vowed to see the world as it was. But oh, how the sight of this man, engrossed in the bridge's aura, whisked her into a whimsy! She envisioned him as a seasoned traveler, a sage adorned with tales of love and loss, his wisdom woven into the very fabric of his being. And for a brief, indulgent moment, Clara allowed herself to be swept up in a fantasy where he was the protagonist.

In her daydream, they escaped to her hidden cabin, shrouded by the forest's embrace, a stone's throw from the bridge. Inside, the flicker of candlelight danced on the walls. They swayed in each other's arms, lost in a rhythm meant only for them, on the brink of a kiss that promised more. But reality, with its impeccable timing, had Clara tripping over her own feet, straight into the arms of the very man in her daydreams.

Their eyes locked, his lit with a spark of amusement, while Clara's cheeks blazed with mortification. Her heart pounded—not from the stumble, but from the revelation that her daydreams had crashed into reality. How utterly awkward. The man stepped back, radiating a rugged allure and tender fortitude.

Standing a little over six feet, his deep-set hazel eyes seemed to hold tales she couldn't quite read, but wanted to. The playful tousle in his chestnut hair and sun-kissed complexion spoke of outdoor hours, while the light stubble added a touch of masculinity. She drifted into another daydream where those very hands traced stories on her skin. Clara snapped herself back to the present. *Focus,* she thought with a smirk. Everything was looking like a romance novel.

"I'm so sorry," Clara mumbled, feeling her cheeks heat under his observant look. His laughter, deep and warm, eased the tension, sending an unexpected thrill through her.

"No harm done," he answered. "Seems we were both lost in thought. I'm Jack Thompson."

She grasped his hand, finding reassurance in its firmness. "Clara Mitchell. It's a pleasure."

Their handshake lingered for a moment longer than necessary before she let go. Then, trying to steer the conversation into less flustered waters, she ventured, "Do you come here often?."

Jack answered. "Actually, yes. Its history and architecture have always fascinated me."

That sparked Clara's enthusiasm, her earlier research bubbling to the surface. "You're interested in the legends, too? I'm working on a book and thought the tale of this bridge would be a perfect addition."

His eyebrows raised. "'This bridge' has a name, you know. But let me guess, you're thinking of including Willows Bridge?"

Clara was surprised. "Isn't that its name?"

He shook his head. "It's actually called the Gold Brook Bridge, built back in 1844. But I agree, 'Willows Bridge' has a pleasant sound to it."

She smiled. "It seems the local legends have more charm than the real name."

He laughed, nodding. "That's often the case. Sometimes the stories can be more compelling than the facts."

"That's what they pay me for," Clara grinned.

The conversation flowed from there, the initial awkwardness melting away as they found common ground in their shared interest. They talked about the history of the bridge, its architectural significance, and the tragic love story that gave it its infamous name. The more they chatted, the clearer it became that there was an undeniable chemistry between them. The universe, it seemed, had thrown them together at this moment, and neither was in a hurry to pull away.

As they stood side by side, overlooking the expanse, Jack described its architectural intricacies with genuine passion. "The way these beams intersect and hold the weight, it's a marvel. It's sturdy, designed to last decades, but even a minor flaw can lead to a collapse."

Clara's eyes lit up. "It sounds like relationships. Built to endure, but they can be so fragile, can't they?"

Jack looked at her with surprise. "That's an interesting analogy. You have a way with words. What sort of book are you working on? I would almost peg you as a poet."

She chuckled, her blue eyes dancing with mischief. "Close, but not quite. I'm a novelist. Mostly mysteries and paranormal stuff. And you? With your knowledge of bridges, I'd guess... an architect?"

Jack laughed, "Not quite, but you're in the ballpark. I'm a structural engineer. I work with structures, designs, the nitty-gritty details."

The revelation seemed to draw them even closer. Two individuals from opposite worlds, yet finding a connection.

"I bet this bridge has seen countless stories," Clara mused, leaning over the railing, her eyes dreamy. "Lovers meeting in secret, teary goodbyes, and ghosts..."

Jack raised an eyebrow, amused. "Ghosts? You're referring to Anne of the Willows, aren't you?"

"Absolutely!" Clara leaned forward. "A tragic love story ending in heartbreak on this very bridge. They say her spirit still lingers. You come here a lot. Have you ever seen it?"

"The spirit?" Jack shook his head, smiling. "I've been here many times, even late at night, and never once felt any presence. The tales are entertaining, but I'm a man of science. Ghosts are a bit out of my realm."

She tilted her head with a teasing smile. "You don't have even the slightest belief in the supernatural? The unexplained mysteries of the world?" Her eyes sparkled as she added, "It gives life a certain... mystique, don't you think?"

He chuckled, brushing a hand through his hair. "Mystique or not, I've always been the kind to trust facts over fantasies."

Clara leaned in, the playful glint still clear. "Well, while you were up late in college, lost in your equations and drafts, I wandered the world through my stories. Ever been to Morocco?"

Jack shook his head. "Never, but I bet you're going to tell me a story from there."

With a nod, she spun a tale of bustling markets and moonlit desert nights. He responded with an amusing recount of an engineering mishap during a project.

The sun had passed its zenith, marking the passage of time they seemed oblivious to.

Jack mused, "You know, a story set right here *would* be fascinating."

Clara chuckled. "I might just feature a skeptic engineer who ends up falling hopelessly in love with a ghost."

"That would be quite the story," Jack said with a wide grin. "Just make sure he's as charming as he is skeptical."

"Absolutely," Clara replied with a wink. "Imagine the tales this bridge could inspire on a day like this."

Jack's lowered as he touched Clara's shoulder, "With the way you tell stories, you'd have anyone believing in ghosts and hidden treasures by dinner."

Their laughter faded as they shared a moment. A spark kindled between them. Clara, caught up in the excitement, paused when she noticed a faint line on Jack's hand—a ring that had once been there.

The atmosphere shifted as reality seeped in. Clara's heart sank. "Are you married?"

Jack met her gaze, the lightness in his eyes giving way to a somber reflection. "Was. It's over now, though," he said. A slight edge hinted at a deeper story.

An awkward silence filled with a flurry of unasked questions and emotions—surprise, curiosity, and disappointment. Clara wondered about the significance of the ring mark. Did it represent a lingering attachment, or perhaps a difficulty in moving on?

Jack seemed to catch her look. He touched the spot where the ring had been, a thoughtful expression on his face. "It's been tough," he admitted. "But I'm being honest with you."

He changed the subject. "Ever looked into the history of this bridge? Or the town itself?"

Clara welcomed the shift in conversation. "Not really. I've been so wrapped up in the legends that I've missed the actual history."

His mood brightened as he launched into an explanation. "This bridge, this town, they're full of history. Way before any legend, this bridge was a marvel of its time. Stowe started in lumber and agriculture, but it was actually one of the first places to have alpine skiing!.."

As Jack shared tales from the town's past, the sun shone brightly overhead, yet something unusual happened. A thick fog rose from the water, enveloping them in a cool mist that seemed out of place in the afternoon warmth.

Clara, caught between listening to Jack and observing the changing environment, couldn't ignore the bridge's transformation. "Is it strange," she asked, "for fog to roll in like this on such a clear day?"

Jack paused, glancing around at the creeping mist. "It adds mystery, doesn't it?" he remarked as the temperature dropped.

Visibility dwindled as the fog thickened. Jack's stories of the founding families and their enduring spirits seemed to breathe life into the mist. Clara's gaze was drawn to the bridge's edge, where she glimpsed what looked like a woman's silhouette within the fog.

"Did you see that?" Clara interrupted. "There, at the edge—it looked like someone was standing there."

Jack looked in the direction she pointed, squinting through the fog. "Maybe we're not the only ones interested in these stories."

Clara was sure she saw the same faint silhouette of a woman the day before. It wasn't solid, more like a wisp of smoke, yet human. Her heart raced, recalling the sensation she had felt. "Whatever or whoever it was... They're gone."

Jack offered a comforting smile. "This fog plays tricks on the eyes. And after the stories you've heard about Anne, it's only natural to think you're seeing things."

But Clara wasn't convinced. "It felt so real. Like she was right there, just out of reach."

Jack hesitated for a moment. "Let's head back," he suggested. "It's getting late, and this fog isn't helping."

Clara could still feel the coolness left behind by the bridge's chill, even as they moved away from it. The atmosphere felt charged, and there was an unspoken acknowledgment between them about the strangeness of the afternoon.

"Is your car parked nearby?" Jack asked, breaking the silence that had settled between them.

She shook her head, her eyes still taking him in. "I walked. I'm staying in a cabin not too far from here."

Something flickered in Jack's eyes. "Same here. Well, the walking part. Which way are you headed?"

She pointed down a path, her gaze drifting towards the bridge they'd just left. "That way."

Jack paused, his guarded for a split second, making her wonder what he hid more beneath the surface. "I'm headed the opposite way, but I've lived in Stowe all my life. Mind if I walk you home?"

She found comfort in his protective offer. "I'd like that. Thank you."

Best to shift the conversation away from the bridge and the unexpected pull she felt towards him. "Tell me more about your work."

Jack's face lit up, his guard dropping. "By day, I'm an engineer, but bridges, especially these historical ones, are my passion. Every bridge in New England tells a story, both of its construction and of the souls that have crossed t hem."

He handed her a sketchbook filled with detailed depictions of bridges. Clara was impressed. "These are incredible," she said.

Their fingers met as they turned the pages together, the connection between them undeniable. Lost in shared appreciation, the world around them faded away.

As the two journeyed deeper into the woods, an understanding seemed to form. Yet, with every step, Jack's walls seemed to grow taller, and Clara found herself more intrigued by the man beside her.

When they reached Clara's cabin, she posed a question to break the growing silence. "What do people around here do for fun?"

With a chuckle, Jack responded, "This is primarily a ski town. But there's a local bar nearby with live music on weekends. You might enjoy it."

The pause that followed was loaded, their respective pasts clear. Jack hesitated, then handed her a scribbled note. "In case you ever want to talk... about bridges or otherwise."

She hesitated and shook her head. "Jack...," she began, but the words seemed to elude her.

He nodded in understanding. "Just in case."

The sadness in his eyes spoke volumes, but he tried to lighten the mood. "Good luck, Clara Mitchell. I truly hope our paths cross again."

She offered a small, rueful smile. "Thank you, Jack."

Inside her cabin, Clara made her way to an armchair, letting the cushioned comfort envelop her. As she settled, the day replayed in her mind. Jack's confident stride, his uninhibited laughter, the way his eyes seemed to pierce right through her defenses. She couldn't deny the chemistry they shared. It had been intoxicating. In another life, she mused, she might've thrown caution to the wind and let the night take its course with him.

A soft sigh escaped her lips. She wanted an escape that might let her forget, even just the emotional baggage she carried. It would've been easy to let him in, to lose herself in a brief whirlwind of connection.

Yet, as inviting as the idea was, the reality lurked nearby. Jack's marriage, recent and raw, was a clear red flag. She herself was no stranger to heartbreak. Tenderness and scars mingled in her past, reminding her to tread carefully. And beyond all that personal history, Boston awaited her return, with its busy streets and bustling life.

She leaned back, squeezing her eyes shut. Hell, she hadn't been looking for some deep, soul-stirring connection. The intensity she felt with Jack was almost too much. She didn't need another romantic saga ending in tragedy. But of course, life didn't always play by the rules.

Ethan, with his erratic behaviors and moods, had brought both excitement and chaos into her life. That unpredictability, once exhilarating, had also been the root of their downfall. But Jack? His entire demeanor was different–grounded, mature, stable. It was as if he bore his experiences, but wore them like armor. That adult vibe about him, the composed facade with storms beneath. It hinted at depths and passions Clara wanted to explore. It made her wonder about the man behind those thoughtful eyes. What experiences had shaped him? How had they made him into who he was today? And, even if she wouldn't admit it aloud, it made her wonder what kind of lover he might be. Would he carry that same intensity, the same purpose and presence into more intimate situations?

After spending the afternoon engrossed in her work, Clara felt the day's efforts weigh on her. The evening's quietude pressed, signaling it was time to wind down. Yet, as she started her nighttime routine, a peculiar sensation interrupted the serenity of the cabin. An unsettling chill slithered through the rooms, insidious and unexpected. Her breath materialized as frosty puffs in the space. The room felt stripped of its coziness, overtaken by a cold malevolence that seemed to seep from the very walls. This abrupt shift from a day filled with productiveness to an evening charged with an eerie discomfort left Clara unnerved.

A book, which had rested on the shelf, now teetered at its edge. Without warning, it plummeted to the ground, landing with a thud that echoed in the stillness. Shadows contorted, their forms darkening and twisting as if animated by some unseen force.

Whispers then interrupted the oppressive silence. These soft murmurs amplified, yet never quite discernible. Like tendrils of smoke, they encircled Clara, faint cries hinting at old sorrows and betrayals. She shook her head, trying to scatter the sounds, chiding herself for letting her imagination take the reins. But her self-composure wavered when she felt a sharp sting on her arm. To her horror, a raw scratch stared back at her.

Clara's heart raced as she stumbled into the kitchen. The icy embrace of the freezer greeted her, revealing a bottle of vodka left by the last renter. Its surface was covered in a frosty sheen that seemed to glint mockingly at her. Memories of her struggles with alcohol surged forward, casting shadows over her recent victories. In a moment of panic, her fingers sought the comforting weight of her AA coin in her pocket, only to find emptiness.

That coin was more than just a piece of metal. It was her anchor. The absence of this touchstone sent a chill through her, deeper than the cold air from the freezer. It left her feeling adrift, vulnerable to the whims of fate, or perhaps facing a critical test of her resilience.

Torn, Clara hesitated. Despite her inner turmoil, the allure proved irresistible. "Just this once," she murmured, succumbing to the temptation. She poured the drink, its chill a contrast to the warm burn as it slid down her throat.

She allowed herself another glass, the heavy silence of the house wrapping around her like a shroud. When she retreated to her bedroom, the atmosphere seemed charged with an eerie sensation, as if the shadows themselves were alive. Was it the spirit of Anne?

As Clara collapsed onto her bed, the room spinning, she felt enveloped by Anne's history and her escalating fears. Seeking refuge, she drew the covers close, yearning for protection from the unseen forces she sensed were at play. The bed seemed to confine her, intensifying the sensation of being watched.

Clara's mind raced. The presence of Anne's spirit, whether borne of jealousy or as a forewarning, seemed so close.

In this state of vulnerability, the line between reality and the supernatural blurred. Clara drifted into sleep, where the lives of her and Anne intertwined in a dream, their spirits connecting across centuries, bound by shared emotions and unspoken fears.

Chapter Three

Anne's Descent

The relentless rays of the morning sun wormed their way through the gaps in the curtains, illuminating the disarray of Clara's room and casting a harsh spotlight onto her weary face. She groaned, shielding her eyes with one hand, while attempting to prop herself up with the other. Her body felt heavy, laden with the sins of the previous night's excess. This feeling was a familiar foe, an echo of past regrets that Clara had hoped to leave behind. The brief escape provided by the alcohol now seemed a hollow victory.

In the cold light of day, the relief she sought only sharpened the edges of her reality. The vodka's embrace had turned into a reminder of her vulnerability to old habits, her struggle with the siren call of alcohol. The decision to drink, made in a moment of weakness, now weighed on her, a reminder of her ongoing battle with addiction..

This moment laid bare the incessant internal conflict between the desire to escape her reality and the need to confront it. She gave in and abandoned the arduous journey towards healing, tempted her with its simplicity. In this raw and unguarded state, Clara's resolve wavered, teetering on resignation. Yet, it was this very confrontation that ignited a spark of resilience within her. Despite the allure of surrender, a part of her clung to the belief that the fight for sobriety, however grueling, held meaning. This sliver of hope suggested that perhaps the true measure of strength lay not in never falling, but in the courage to rise.

She moved out to the living room, trying to shake off the weariness. The local books and magazines on the coffee table caught her blurry attention. She flipped through them. One particular title stood out — *Haunted Vermont*. Curiosity piqued, she opened it to a random page, and a headline: Willows Bridge captured her gaze. This seemed to be the same article she had found in the magazine in Boston. It appeared the universe still wanted her to tell Anne's story.

She settled more comfortably into the plush couch cushions and read:

The Mysterious Tale of Anne Wentworth: A Haunted Vermont Chronicle

In the landscapes of Vermont, where history seeps from the cobblestone streets and ghostly legends lurk in the shadows, the tragic story of Anne Wentworth remains a mystery, transcending time. Born on November 16, 1846, and tragically passing away on June 13, 1866, Anne's life and untimely death are woven into the state's haunted past.

A Love Story Shrouded in Mystery

The mid-19th century, a period marked by the glow of gaslights and the clip-clop of horse-drawn carriages, sets the stage for our tale. This period, characterized by its rigid adherence to tradition and the sanctity of family honor, serves as the backdrop to a tale of forbidden love that defies the era's stringent societal norms.

Anne Wentworth, born into a wealthy family renowned for its thriving lumber business, was the epitome of grace and ambition, her spirit unbound by the conventions of her time. Despite being nurtured in an environment where lineage and wealth dictated one's future, Anne's outlook remained untainted by cynicism. Her heart was a reservoir of dreams, brimming with optimism and a fervent passion for life that distinguished her from her contemporaries.

In the heart of this Vermont town, fate orchestrated Anne and Thomas's introduction. He was a young stable hand whose modest upbringing stood opposite to Anne's affluent background. This encounter ignited a flame of attraction that neither societal boundaries nor the dictates of class could extinguish. Their love, though forbidden, blossomed in the shadows, nurtured by the secrecy that enveloped their union. Beneath the watchful eyes of a society that would never approve, their bond deepened. Each clandestine rendezvous, each stolen kiss, and every tender whisper part of a shared dream—a dream of a life together, unshackled by the chains of social expectation.

Yet, the very essence of their connection—cast a long shadow over their hopes. This juxtaposition of worlds, one of privilege and the other of simplicity, set the stage for a love story that remains etched in the annals of Vermont's haunted history.

Tragedy at the Bridge

As is often the case, the brighter the flame, the darker the shadow it casts. Anne's joy soon turned to despair upon discovering she was with child, a development that threatened to bring disgrace to her family and ostracize her from society. Undeterred, the lovers hatched a daring plan: they would rendezvous at the old bridge at midnight, whence they would flee to a nearby town and start anew, free from the burdens of judgment and scorn.

The stage was set for their escape, but as the appointed hour approached, an eerie calm settled over the bridge. Anne, heart pounding with anticipation and fear, waited under the cover of darkness. Yet, as the night stretched on, it became clear that Thomas would not come. The dawn brought with it a devastating realization: Thomas had vanished, leaving Anne alone, vulnerable, and facing an uncertain future.

Overwhelmed by despair and a sense of betrayal, Anne found herself at a crossroads. The thought of returning home, to face the judgment of her family and the stifling constraints of a society that had never been her own, became unbearable. Her isolation and the shattered dreams of a future that would never come to pass engulfed her. In those darkest moments before the sun pierced the horizon, Anne made a heart-wrenching decision. Believing she had nothing left to hold on to and no one to turn to, she stepped off the bridge, seeking solace in the river's embrace rather than endure a life filled with the echoes of her lost love. This tragic act marked the end of Anne Wentworth's story in the physical world, but it was just the beginning of her legend in the haunted annals of Vermont's history.

A Legacy of Haunting

Anne Wentworth's story is a reminder of the enduring power of love and the heartache of betrayal. Her spirit still haunts the old bridge, a sorrowful figure forever waiting for a lover who will never return. To this day, visitors report an inexplicable chill in the air and the faint sound of a woman's sigh carried on the breeze.

Clara felt a shiver crawl up her spine. The tale of Anne Wentworth was filled with a sorrow that seemed to transcend time, making her morning's hangover take a back seat. The story from "Haunted Vermont" lingered in Clara's mind, but it also sparked a surge of inspiration. She ventured out, back to the place it all happened, hoping the fresh air would invigorate her ideas.

As she approached, Clara's heart fluttered, half-hoping to see Jack. Yet, there was no sign of him. The bridge stood empty, surrounded by the chorus of nature.

Finding a secluded spot carpeted with wildflowers, Clara felt it was the perfect setting for her writing. She waited for inspiration, pen poised. But then, an uncanny sensation overtook her—a whisper of fabric, the soft rustle akin to a dress brushing against grass, and an invisible presence that felt like a perfume lingering in the air.

Emotions surged within Clara—anguish, hope, despair—as if she were channeling Anne Wentworth's sentiments from that fateful night. She wrote: "Heart pounding, anticipation sharp as a knife's edge, love and betrayal." Periodically, she paused, sensing an unseen touch or a whisper, yet finding nothing but nature's calm around her.

Her writing captured the yearning, waiting, and the profound sorrow of broken promises. It was as if Anne's spirit guided her hand, pouring the words into Clara from beyond.

As the sun hung in the sky, Clara noticed a glint by the water. Curiosity led her down the slope to the water's edge. A heart-shaped locket, tarnished by time, lay among the pebbles, its age and design giving it with an air of mystery.

With a moment of hesitation, Clara lifted the locket. Could this be Anne's? The idea appeared improbable, yet an undeniable connection lingered. Upon opening it, Clara discovered it was empty. The once-held treasures long faded away. She thought she detected a soft sigh, as if it echoed with whispers from the past. Tucking the locket into her pocket, she glanced at the sky; the afternoon was advancing, and she had no desire to find herself on the bridge after dark.

After Clara returned to her cabin, a sense of anticipation engulfed her. The retreat offered the perfect backdrop for introspection and creative work and she found herself compelled to explore the haunting saga of Anne Wentworth through this locket. There was an intrinsic connection between herself and the tangible piece of history she cradled in her hands.

Under the soft illumination of the cabin lights, Clara embarked on a delicate task. She prepared a simple cleaning solution, combining baking soda and salt, and placed the aged locket within it. With care, she scrubbed away years of tarnish, revealing a luster that had been obscured by time's relentless march. The act felt almost ceremonial, as if she were peeling back the layers of Anne's story. Once the locket regained its sheen, Clara threaded it onto a chain she often wore and put it around her neck.

As the evening shadows played along the walls, Clara's thoughts were adrift in a sea of memories that were not her own. She envisioned cobblestone streets alive with laughter, secret glances shared under the guise of night, and the unbearable pressure of societal expectations. The emotional turmoil of a young woman's heart, buoyed by hope and then shattered by betrayal, was something very real to Clara.

The locket's cold press against her chest seemed to beat in tandem with another's heart, bridging centuries. The sight of the empty vodka bottle, a reminder of her recent backslide, spurred a moment of introspection. Clara rationalized this lapse as a mere vacation misstep and promised to resume her sobriety when she returned to real life, yet

considered the idea of allowing herself just one drink during her next visit to town.

Clara touched the locket, and it served as a conduit,
whisking her away from the confines of the cabin and
into the past. She found herself enveloped in a whirlwind
of emotions, offering her a glimpse into the nuances of
betrayal, love, and fleeting happiness—a scene that seemed
to plead for a voice.

Suddenly, Clara was standing in a barn, the scent of hay
mingling with the symphony of distant crickets. Before
her, in the warm glow of a lantern, stood two figures
caught in a clandestine rendezvous.

Anne's cheeks were tinged with excitement and trepidation. She stood beside a man whose presence was marked
by a quiet intensity.

"Thomas," Anne whispered.

Thomas gazed into Anne's eyes and cradled her face in
his hands. "Anne," he replied, his voice thick with feeling, "here and now, it's only us. Nothing else matters."

"I'm frightened. What if we're discovered?"

He soothed her, his thumb caressing her cheek. "Trust
me, Anne, in this moment, we're all that exists. I wish for
nothing more than to be by your side, always."

Hesitation flickered across Anne's face as she gripped his
hand. "But if someone sees... The sin of it all..."

Thomas removed her bonnet, unleashing her hair to cascade. "My dear Anne," he murmured, tucking a strand behind her ear, "Forget the world outside."

Their connection deepened with a kiss. As they embraced, shedding the layers of societal expectations along with their outer garments, their passion was tangible.

Caught in the moment's intensity, Clara felt as though she was experiencing Anne's emotions firsthand. The memory was vivid, saturated with the longing and tenderness of their union.

Yet, as Clara remained a silent observer, a sense of foreboding encroached. The shadow of impending heartbreak that loomed over Anne's story pulled Clara back into her own reality, leaving her heart heavy.

She gasped for air, her heart pounding as she yanked the locket from around her neck. The moment it broke free, the vision of Anne's world released its hold on her. The locket, now disconnected, tumbled from her fingers and hit the drawer with a clatter.

As she settled back against the couch, her head throbbed from the experience. "I really need to unwind. Maybe find a little adventure." Her gaze drifted to the empty vodka bottle on the counter, taunting her with memories of the night before. The desire for another escape gnawed at her.

The shadows transformed ordinary corners and spaces into mysterious hideaways. Clara was terrified. With increasing desperation, she scoured every conceivable place where the owner might have hidden a bottle. She rummaged through the cabinets, the refrigerator, even the unlikeliest of spots.

After taking a steadying breath, Clara turned to her laptop for a solution. A quick search pointed her to the bar Jack had told her about. Relief was just a short stroll away. She threw on a sweatshirt and headed for the door, her thoughts already on escaping the confines of her temporary retreat.

As she headed toward the bar, she tried to push away the voices in her head.

This isn't you anymore. Remember the promises? The AA tokens? The late-night crying bouts swearing never again?

But another voice chimed in, louder, more insistent. *It's just a drink. You deserve a moment of reprieve. You're on vacation anyway, remember?*

As she walked, the fresh air seemed to clear her head. The streetlights painted an eerie glow on the path, and with each step, Anne's presence seemed to lighten.

It's just one drink to help with the stress, Clara reasoned. *The story, Ethan, this place, the memories from that damn locket. A drink, one drink, to calm the nerves, and then you can get to writing.*

By the time she reached the bar, her resolve had weakened. The door's chime as she entered was almost drowned out by her internal justifications. *It's different this time. Just one to take the edge off. I'll handle it.*

The bar radiated an old-world charm, its walls darkened by decades of memories. Antique bulbs lent the space a rich, golden glow. An acoustic band was setting up on the stage. As the lead guitarist adjusted his instrument, Clara's heart missed a beat. There was something in the way he moved, the tilt of his head, that reminded her of Ethan. The similarity wasn't exact, but the resemblance was uncanny.

A pang of longing coupled with an urgent desire to forget surged through her. She scanned the bar, her eyes darting from one face to another, searching for someone interesting, someone who might offer a momentary escape. The thrill of a diversion she felt she needed and deserved.

Clara signaled the bartender. "Whiskey, neat," she ordered. The first sip was sharp, a welcomed sting.

The bar's atmosphere buzzed with subdued conversations and anticipation of the evening's performance. As Clara's eyes locked onto the man a few stools away. Tall and with a lean build, there was a magnetic energy about him. The way the fabric of his shirt stretched across his well-defined arms, hinting at hours spent at the gym, sent her mind wandering. Perhaps he'd be the remedy for the evening's growing restlessness.

"Going with whiskey, huh?" The deep timbre of his voice sent a shiver down her spine.

She glanced back at her empty stool and quipped, "Is that a recommendation?"

With a smile that hinted at shared secrets, he replied, "From one connoisseur to another, it's a good choice."

She arched an eyebrow. "Is that so?"

He chuckled, a warm, infectious sound that drew her in even more. "Name's Leo."

"Clara."

As Clara was about to continue the playful banter, a cheerful voice from her other side interrupted her thoughts. "Hey there! Mind if I join you?" A girl with bright eyes and an even brighter smile introduced herself. "I'm Jess."

Surprised, Clara nodded and motioned for her to take the empty seat beside her. Just as Jess began sharing a story about her day, Leo's presence became more pronounced.

Without a word, he handed her a glass filled with amber liquid.

"Top-shelf," he said with a wink, "on me."

As the second drink slid in front of her, Clara lifted it in acknowledgment. "Don't mind if I do," she murmured, letting the rich aroma of the whiskey tantalize her senses. She took a slow sip and let the smooth liquid roll over her tongue. Her gaze locked with Leo's, and with a seductive glint in her eyes, she gave a soft, "thank you."

As the third drink arrived, the night swayed and the edge of her vision blurred just enough to make her feel light and free. This was what she needed.

"Dance?" Leo asked, extending a hand.

"Why not?" She took Leo's outstretched hand and allowed him to lead her to the dance floor. As they moved in rhythm, the world around them seemed to sink into a hazy background. The feel of Leo's powerful hands on her waist sent a shiver up her spine. As he pulled her closer, the contours of her body molded against his, their movements synchronizing. This would do.

After the song, they headed back to the bar. "How about a shot to keep the rhythm going?" Leo suggested with a playful grin.

"Don't mind if I do," Clara replied.

All of a sudden, Jess was there, her presence exuding a unique energy that Clara hadn't noticed earlier. "Mind if I steal her?" Jess's voice was playful as she spoke over the music, wrapping an arm around Clara's waist. The unexpected touch sent a jolt of electricity through Clara, her skin tingling under Jess's fingers.

While Clara had been with mostly men in the past, she wasn't unfamiliar with the pull of attraction toward a woman. Her heart rate quickened, her mind racing to process the whirlwind of emotions. She hadn't entertained the idea of being with Jess tonight, but in that fleeting moment, the thought held a certain appeal.

Before long, Leo joined them. As the trio danced, their moves became more synchronized, their laughter blending into the music. The intimacy of the dance, combined with the alcohol coursing through her veins, made the world seem distant. Time seemed to lose its meaning, and all that mattered was the music and the electrifying connection.

Their playful rivalry for Clara's attention, the alternating warmth of Leo's touch and the soft caresses of Jess, left Clara elated. The push and pull, the ebb and flow of their interactions, heightened her senses. The closeness, the hot breaths, the shared laughter—all of it conspired to draw Clara deeper into the moment, her inhibitions melting aw ay.

Jess took Clara's hand, her fingers intertwining, giving a tug. "Come with me," she said. The two made their way through the crowd, with Leo following close behind, and Jess pushed open the door to the bathroom, ushering Clara in.

The world seemed a little distant as the door shut and Jess clicked the lock. Sounds from the bar, the more immediate ambiance of water dripping, their synchronized breaths, and the occasional muffled laughter that penetrated the walls replaced the hum of conversation.

The bathroom's overhead lights painted the three in alternating shades of gold and shadow. As Leo removed his jacket, the contours of his muscular form became more pronounced. His woodsy fragrance filled the room. As Clara's vision wavered and the pain in her head became too much to bear, a flash of realization pierced the fog of confusion. This wasn't just alcohol. But the thought was fleeting. She was being swallowed by the overpowering sensations that held her captive.

"Maybe... maybe we should go back," she murmured.

Before Clara could take another step, Jess's hand captured hers. "Not yet," Jess whispered, her gaze locked onto Clara's.

The walls of the bathroom seemed to shift and spin, the dim lights appearing as hazy streaks in Clara's blurred vision. A sudden wave of lightheadedness washed over her, causing her legs to wobble and buckle beneath her. As the ground rushed up to meet her, she felt herself falling; the world turning dark around the edges.

In the fog, Jess and Leo exchanged a quick glance, their previous playfulness replaced with the precision of those familiar with such situations. They moved in tandem, their actions choreographed from experiences.

With a swift, well-rehearsed grace, Jess unzipped Clara's purse, her fingers searching its contents. "Wallet's on the left," Leo said.

Jess nodded, pulling out the wallet with ease. She handed it over to Leo, who slipped it into his pocket with a deftness that spoke of many repetitions.

As Clara's head lolled, her drugged state pulling her further into unconsciousness; she watched Jess and Leo shared one last glance. There was no guilt in their eyes, just a cool detachment.

Adjusting their clothes with practiced efficiency, they left the bathroom as silently as they had entered, merging into the bar's crowd, leaving a vulnerable Clara behind in their wake.

The bathroom seemed to pulsate, intensifying the throbbing in her head and the chilled tiles beneath her provided a jarring contrast to the growing warmth creeping up her face. All the scents—a mix of cleaning agents, spilled drinks, and an undercurrent of sweat—turned her stomach.

Every sound felt magnified, the knocking on the door sounding like thunderclaps in her ears. But above all, a voice, insistent and growing anxious, permeated her foggy senses. "Clara? Clara, are you in there?"

She tried to move, to respond, but her limbs felt like they were anchored. The weight of her eyelids was almost too much to bear, but she fought to keep them open, desperate for some tether to reality.

The door burst open, letting in a flood of ambient bar noise—the muffled beat of a song, distant laughter, the clinking of glasses. A figure stood in the doorway, backlit, casting a shadow over her. As her eyes adjusted, the familiar contours of a face came into focus.

"Jack..." she whispered, her voice sounding far away even to her own ears.

His eyes darted over her form. "Oh, Clara," Jack breathed out, rushing to her side. "What the hell happened?" She tried to answer, but before anything came out, the world went black.

The moon cast long shadows on the winding road that led to the bridge, painting a haunting silhouette of the girl as she walked. With every step, her secret grew heavier, a life growing inside her, the love that was supposed to be eternal, yet now tainted with betrayal.

She could hear the whispers of the villagers even in their absence, their judgmental voices forming a storm inside her head. The world seemed to blur and stretch, reality and her darkest fears becoming indistinguishable.

The bridge's truss seemed to beckon her and the girl hesitated for a moment, feeling the tiny flutter of life inside her. This reminder of her unborn child only intensified the shame and anguish she felt. She thought of the child growing within her, innocent yet already bearing her sins and society's judgment.

With rain beginning to fall, mirroring her tears, she approached the bridge. The water below roared, a tumultuous chorus to her internal storm. She leaned over the rail and whispered a soft apology to the life within her.

Clara, suspended between the realms of the conscious and unconscious, felt Anne's torment suffocating her. She could hear the faint heartbeat of Anne's unborn child, echoing the rhythm of her own pulse. The shared pain, the shame, the desperate acts of a soul tormented by love intertwined in Clara's mind, reminding her of the fragile threads that connect all human experiences.

CHAPTER FOUR

Distracting Desires

Clara's eyelids fluttered open, her headache pressing down like an anchor. A sharp sting pierced her temples, making the light that seeped through the curtains feel almost blinding. As she shifted beneath the covers, the textures and scents of her bedding felt uncomfortable. Confusion gnawed at her, intertwining with the remnants of a hazed intoxication. The room should have offered comfort, but it intensified her disorientation. How did she end up back in her own bed? She had no memory of returning home.

Clara forced herself to sit upright as she gritted her teeth against the throbbing in her head. Every movement sent fresh waves of nausea surging through her, making the room tilt. With a shaky hand, she brushed stray strands of hair from her face and swung her legs over the side of the bed.

The events of the previous night felt like distorted fragments of a dream — disconnected and surreal. Her clothes, creased and smelling of stale cigarettes and alcohol, clung to her skin. A flood of shame washed over her as the memory of drink after drink dominated her mind.

With a heavy sigh, she muttered, "Never again." It just wasn't worth it. She slipped out of her soiled outfit and reached for the nearest clean t-shirt. After pulling it over her head, she followed with a pair of sweatpants.

Then, steeling herself against the pounding in her head, Clara made her way to the kitchen. The thought of a strong cup of coffee became a singular focus, driving her forward, each step steadier than the last.

Just as she reached for the coffeepot, a shadowy movement in her peripheral vision sent her heart racing. Panic flared as the memory of the locket flooded her brain. In a split second of pure instinct, she scanned the countertops for anything she could use as a weapon. Her hand landed on a wooden spatula.

But as she whirled around, spatula raised and ready to strike, her eyes met a familiar, if unexpected, face: Jack.

"Whoa, hey! It's just me," he exclaimed, raising his hands in a placating gesture.

Clara's posture sagged with relief, the spatula now feeling absurd in her hand. She placed it back on the counter, her pulse still racing. Then she cleared her throat. "So, um... what are you doing in my house?"

Jack took a deep breath and leaned against the kitchen island, his gaze averted, as if searching for the right words. "I saw you last night at the bar," he began, his voice gentle.

She frowned, trying to recall. "You did?"

He nodded, his dark eyes searching hers. "I went over to say hello, but... you looked preoccupied. I didn't want to intrude."

Clara's cheeks flushed, embarrassment seeping in as fragmented memories attempted to piece together. "I... don't remember much after my third drink," she admitted.

Jack's expression turned serious. "Yeah, I noticed. That's why I kept an eye on you. That couple you were with, they acted... off."

"Off? How?"

He hesitated, choosing his words. "They seemed too familiar with you, considering you'd just met. They were constantly by your side, watching your every move. It made me uncomfortable." Jack paused, rubbing the back of his neck. "When I saw you go to the bathroom with them, I had a bad feeling. Then you never came back out."

Clara's eyes widened in shock, the implications of Jack's words dawning on her. "And then... what happened?"

Jack shifted, his cheeks tinged red. "When they came out, they seemed... oddly composed, given the situation. I watched them whisper to each other, and something about it didn't feel right." He coughed. "So, I checked the bathroom."

A lump formed in Clara's throat as realization dawned on her. "That's how you found me..."

He nodded. "You were out of it. I didn't want to leave you there, so I brought you home."

Clara took a shaky breath, her cheeks flushing a deeper shade of red. The mortification of being seen in such a state, especially by Jack, was almost unbearable. She was used to being the responsible one in her relationships, despite her occasional lapses into excess. And yet here she was, being cared for by someone who clearly had his life together far better than she did.

She looked at him. "I've been trying to control my drinking," she admitted. "Last night was a relapse. I just wanted to forget everything for a while."

Jack's gaze held understanding, perhaps even familiarity. "I've been there," he replied.

Clara perked up, a question forming on her lips. "You have?"

For a moment, a shadow passed over Jack's eyes, and he seemed to retreat within himself. "It's not something I talk about," he said, avoiding her gaze.

Jack cleared his throat and shifted on his feet. "Look, I don't want to be the bearer of bad news so early, but... they got away with your wallet."

Clara's heart sank, and her headache intensified. "Oh, shit!" She groaned. "I have to cancel all my cards. My driver's license was in there... everything."

Jack ran a hand through his disheveled hair. "I did my best. By the time I got to you, they'd vanished into the crowd. I made sure you were safe, though, and reported the theft to the police."

The ache in Clara's head dulled as she processed Jack's words. His rugged appearance was only made more captivating by his obvious concern.

"Oh no," she replied, shaking her head, her voice quivering. "It's not your fault, Jack. It's mine. I... I shouldn't have put myself in that position." She hesitated, meeting his gaze with vulnerable sincerity. "I appreciate everything you did for me. I can't thank you enough."

Jack shifted. "You don't have to thank me. I just did what felt right."

She winced, memories from the night attempting to resurface. The fragmented snippets played in her mind: dim bar lights, the press of bodies, the heady mix of alcohol, and a dizzying whirl of emotions. She drew in a shuddering breath. "God, I can't believe I let this happen," she said, pressing the heels of her hands into her temples, trying to wish away both the headache and the shame of the night.

"It's not your fault," Jack assured her. "People can be opportunistic. But I promise, we'll do everything we can to sort this out."

When she met his gaze, Clara felt a rush of gratitude, intertwined with the sting of her own self-imposed humiliation. She murmured a soft, "Thank you."

Jack hesitated. "Do you want me to leave?"

She bit her lip. "No, please stay. I mean, unless you have to be somewhere?"

Jack smiled. "Honestly, right now, there's no place I'd rather be than here, making sure you're okay."

His composure made her feel a little better as she went over how to get a new copy of her license and which cards she would need to cancel. A sudden knock on the door interrupted their process. Clara tensed up, and Jack moved in front of her, protective.

She opened the door and was met by a stern-looking man with a badge. "Morning, ma'am. I'm Sheriff Daniels. I believe this belongs to you?" He extended her wallet.

She grabbed the wallet, feeling a rush of relief as she flipped it open to ensure its contents were intact. "Oh my God, thank you!" she said, feeling tears prick her eyes.

Sheriff Daniels nodded, his eyes scanning the room and landing on Jack. "We pulled over a couple just outside Burlington last night. Found a bunch of stolen items, yours included. They've been at this for a while."

Clara gasped, "So, this wasn't just random?"

Jack scowled. "Those jerks."

The sheriff added, "If you wouldn't mind, ma'am, we'd like you to come by the station in the next few days to give a statement."

She nodded. "Of course, and thank you."

Jack stepped in closer, his hand finding a reassuring spot on her back. "Thanks, Sheriff. We really appreciate how quickly you're handling this."

As they watched the sheriff's car pull away, the dust swirling behind it on the gravel driveway seemed to pause time itself, bringing Clara back to the here and now. She tried to shift the conversation to lighter territory. "It's so cute here. You've always been in this town?"

Jack's face took on a faraway look. "Born and raised. Left for college, spent some years in Providence. But I found my way back after reconnecting with my high school sweetheart."

"Oh?" Clara wondered if this was his ex. "Is she still in town?"

Jack hesitated for a fraction of a second. "Lila... Yeah, she's still around."

"Lila... is she...?"

Jack, catching the hint, said, "Yes, she's the ex-wife."

A silence fell over them for a moment, and Clara, realizing she might have overstepped, mumbled, "I didn't mean to pry."

Jack tried to ease the tension with a half-smile. "It's a small town. If you are here long enough, you would hear it from someone."

The afternoon sun streamed through the kitchen windows, bathing the room in light. Clara, now feeling refreshed, began rummaging through her fridge. "Want a sandwich?" she asked, laying out various fillings.

"Sounds perfect," Jack replied, stepping beside her to assist. They moved around the kitchen in a coordinated dance, sometimes deliberately, sometimes accidentally grazing against each other. With every touch, a charge seemed to pass between them, adding to the electric atmosphere.

As they assembled their sandwiches, Clara thought about earlier. She could still feel the ghost of Jack's touch on her back and his warm breath when he'd leaned in to speak to her. She shook her head to clear her thoughts, focusing on spreading the mayo. He seemed to be lost in thought, glancing her way when he thought she wouldn't notice.

They sat opposite each other, their conversation touching on lighter topics, like favorite vacation spots and hobbies. But even as they chatted and laughed, there was an undeniable pull.

After finishing their lunch, Jack stretched, breaking the spell for a moment. "I should get going," he said, sounding somewhat hesitant.

Clara nodded, trying to keep her tone neutral. "Thanks for everything today."

His gaze met hers. "It was my pleasure."

He stood at the open door and turned to say his goodbyes. But as he looked down at Clara, the intensity in her eyes was unmistakable. The surrounding air grew heavy.

Jack took a half-step closer, the gap between them shrinking to a breath. Clara's chest heaved, the pulse at the base of her throat racing. Her skin felt like it was on fire, every nerve ending alive. As they held each other's gaze, Jack's breathing became heavier, and for a moment, Clara thought he might close the distance. But with restraint clear in his every move, he murmured a goodbye and stepped back, leaving her in the fading afternoon light.

The silence in the room seemed to amplify once Jack had left. Clara leaned against the door, feeling the coolness of the wood press into her back. She let out a sigh, realizing the strength of the pull between them. *Good thing one of us had some maturity.*

Even with Jack's departure, Clara's heartbeat refused to calm, a familiar pang of yearning echoing within her. Men and alcohol—her two main avenues of escape. She acknowledged the pattern she had sunk into. "I really need to break this cycle," she muttered, glancing in the direction Jack had vanished.

She needed to channel her energy into something productive, and couldn't spend the day pining over what could have been. A glimmer from her desk drawer caught her eye — the locket. It held so many questions, and perhaps the answers were the perfect distraction she needed, and she knew just the person who could help.

Ashlyn Alden.

Clara's debut novel had been a bestseller- landing her a lucrative five book deal with the publisher. Her second manuscript did not come as easily—a thriller entwined with elements of the supernatural—and was proved to be more challenging than she had expected. She needed authenticity, a way to breathe life into the paranormal aspects of her story without veering into overused tropes.

She had heard of Ashlyn through the grapevine of her writing circle—a psychic known not only for her abilities but also for her willingness to consult on creative projects. Taking a leap of faith, Clara reached out, and to her surprise, Ashlyn had been intrigued by her proposal.

The day they met, the air was dark and dreary with winter just giving way to spring. Clara entered the cozy, book-laden study where Ashlyn welcomed her clients. The walls were lined with shelves filled with old tomes and modern works on the supernatural and the aroma of sage lingered in the air. Ashlyn greeted her with a warm, knowing smile, as if she had been expecting Clara all along.

"Clara Mitchell, the suspense writer," Ashlyn had said, her voice tinged with amusement. "To what do I owe the pleasure?"

Clara explained her project—a novel centered on a protagonist who could communicate with the dead. She wanted to ensure her portrayal was respectful and grounded in some semblance of reality, or at least believability.

Ashlyn listened, nodding along as Clara outlined her vision. After a moment of contemplation, Ashlyn shared her insights, weaving tales of her experiences with the spiritual realm. She spoke of the delicate veil between the living and the dead, the energies that lingered in places of significance, and the emotional echoes that could sometimes breach the divide.

As Ashlyn described the sensation of connecting with a spirit—the chill that whispered across the skin, the electric tingle of presence, unseen emotions—Clara took fervent notes. The details were gold, the missing pieces she had been searching for to lend her narrative the authenticity it lacked.

"Remember, Clara," Ashlyn had cautioned, her eyes piercing, "the spirit world is not a parlor trick or a plot device. It's a dimension of existence, rich with emotion and a story. Approach it with respect."

That meeting had been a turning point for Clara. Not only did it provide her with the material she needed to break through her writer's block, but it also marked the beginning of an unexpected friendship. Ashlyn's perspectives on the supernatural had opened Clara's mind to possibilities she had never considered, enriching her story-telling in ways she couldn't have imagined.

Clara picked up her phone and scrolled through her contacts, stopping at Ashlyn's. After taking a deep breath, Clara pressed 'call'. She prepared herself for the conversation, hoping it might provide both a distraction and a clue about the locket's mysterious past.

The ring tone echoed through her ears until a calm, familiar voice answered, "Hello?"

"Hi, Ashlyn. It's Clara Mitchell," she began, her voice shaky. "I hope I'm not intruding. I just... I found something, and I need your expertise."

Ashlyn's tone changed to one of curiosity. "Ah, Clara, it's been some time. What seems to be the matter?"

Clara recounted her discovery of the locket and the initials engraved on it. She spoke of the legends of Anne, and the eerie events that had followed its discovery. The whispers, the dreams—everything spilled out in a rush.

Ashlyn listened, her silence punctuated only by occasional hums of interest. "Objects, especially personal ones, can carry strong residual energies. If it's hers and the legends hold any truth, it's entirely possible the locket keeps a part of her essence."

Clara's grip on the phone tightened. "I feel like I'm tapping into something, perhaps memories or emotions. I thought if anyone could help, it would be you."

"It sounds like more than just residual energy." Ashlyn's voice grew contemplative. "Perhaps an active spirit, one trying to communicate its unfinished business."

Silence hung between them for a moment until Clara broke it. "Are you able to help with this one?"

A soft sigh came from the other end. "It's a good thing I'm not too far from Stowe right now. How about I come into town, have a firsthand look at the locket, and see what I can sense?"

Relief washed over Clara. "That would mean a lot to me. Thank you."

"See you soon, Clara. Take care."

With that, Clara ended the call, anticipation and trepidation warring in her chest.

As twilight deepened, painting the room in shades of dusk, Clara sought refuge in her book, the reading lamp casting a cozy bubble of light in the encroaching darkness. Engrossed in a thrilling passage, she was startled by a cold draft that fluttered the pages and sent a shiver cascading down her spine. The room's temperature plummeted, surrounding her in a chilling embrace.

Unease prickled her skin. She rationalized it as the settling of an old house, yet the air felt dense, charged with an unseen presence. It was as if the very space around her was alive and watching her with unseen eyes. The back of her neck tingled, and she could swear she felt the faintest touch of fingers brushing against her skin.

When she scanned the room, Clara found nothing out of the ordinary. Yet, the oppressive atmosphere pressed on her, quickening her pulse. She summoned her bravery and called out, "Is someone there?" Silence followed, the room growing even colder, then suddenly, the feeling lifted, leaving her questioning reality.

As the evening progressed, shadows danced across the walls, and whispers filled the air. She suspected Anne. The presence felt insistent, almost suffocating, as if the walls themselves were trying to communicate. Suddenly, a book flew from the shelf, and a door slammed.

She felt a little less frightened this time, knowing she had Ashlyn to help. Was Anne attempting to convey a message? Clara recalled some of her friends' teachings and prepared to meditate and reach across the veil. But an electrical surge interrupted. The lights blinked.

Now she was feeling a little more fear. Clara abandoned the meditation and instead chanted a protective incantation. "Guardians of light, shield me tonight. Push away spirits, with all your might." She repeated the lines, each repetition more resolute than the last.

The tumult subsided, but a residual sadness lingered, reflecting the turmoil within Clara herself. Thoughts of Jack, their connection, and the unresolved tension of her life in Boston consumed her. She approached the window, where moonlight offered a serene counterpoint to her internal storm. Lost in thought, Clara stood at the crossroads of her past and the uncertain promise of the future, the night's beauty bittersweet as she pondered the cost of a love that might never be hers.

Tales of the Spirits

The quaint cafe was Clara's chosen hideaway, a refuge from her relentless internal monologue. Tossing and turning the previous night, her mind had been full of thoughts about Jack. Did he distance himself because of her penchant for alcohol and wild nights? Was it the contrasting worlds they came from? The worst part? Realizing how deeply she cared about him. The act of admitting to herself that she was interested had been a harsh wake-up call. She wished she could switch off those feelings, make things simpler.

She hoped Ashlyn might be the distraction she needed. The ambience was comforting, filled with muted chatter and the inviting scent of coffee. Its eclectic furniture, each piece carrying a tale of its own, added to its charm. The day's sunlight wove through the windows, painting everything in a rainbow of colors. But even as she appreciated these details, Clara was aware of her purpose.

Then, a chime from the entrance pulled her from her reverie. Framed by the door stood a figure, illuminated and looking like she stepped out of a dream. Sunlight kissed her dark hair, making it gleam with a celestial sheen. The moment Ashlyn stepped into the room, the entire cafe fell into a hush, all eyes drawn to her. With an air that commanded attention, she seemed to eclipse everything else in the room. For Clara, the background chatter dimmed. All that mattered now was the conversation to come, and the truths it might unveil.

"Clara," Ashlyn greeted her with a smile, her voice soft yet carrying a playfulness and the knowledge that all were watching her. "It feels like forever."

Clara stood, embracing the woman. "It does. I can't believe it's only been a year."

"Time moves differently for people like me, I suppose." Ashlyns laughter filled the air. "Tell me, how have you been?"

"Better to see you," Clara replied with a grin. "And every time I come across 'Grave Secrets' in a bookstore or get a royalty check, I'm reminded of the magic we created together."

Ashlyn waved her hand but with a smile, "Oh, please! Your writing is extraordinary on its own. I just sprinkled stardust, that's all."

Clara leaned in, her tone conspiratorial. "That 'stardust' made all the difference. There is talk of a Netflix Series. The readers couldn't get enough of the paranormal elements you helped infuse. We made quite the team."

"I'm just glad it resonated with so many," Ashlyn replied, her eyes glinting. "But tell me about this thing that has been pulling you back to the realm of the supernatural."

With a sigh, Clara leaned back. "It started with a new story, inspired by a ghost story. It's one you'll find intriguing."

Ashlyn's gaze intensified, signaling her readiness to dive deep once more into the world of spirits and mysteries.

The aroma of baked bread and simmering soups wafted through the cafe. A young waiter approached them, menus in hand. Clara took a moment to peruse the list of hearty dishes before settling on her comfort food of choice, mac and cheese. Ashlyn opted for a creamy tomato basil soup with a side of garlic bread.

As the waiter left with their orders, Clara breathed, her fingers fidgeting with her napkin. "As you know, I didn't call you here just to catch up," she began. "There's been...an occurrence."

Ashlyns's violet eyes focused on Clara. "Go on," she coaxed.

Clara's shoulders dropped, her tension melting away. "I've been experiencing something... haunting. It's a spirit named Anne." She recounted the events that had transpired, the locket's discovery, the dreams, and the increasing sense of urgency and despair she felt.

Ashlynn listened, sipping her soup. Her eyes never left Clara's.

"I feel her pain, her desperation. But every time I try to connect, it just... gets worse." Clara continued.

Ashlyn reached over, covering Clara's hand with her own. The cool touch of her rings sent a calm through Clara. "This spirit, she's trying to convey something important. Something unresolved."

When the waiter dropped off their food, the smell of Clara's mac and cheese filled the air. She pulled up a gooey forkful, and it was like a hug in a bite, giving her normal in the middle of all this ghostly craziness.

Ashlyn broke her garlic bread. "A seance might be the key. To bridge the divide and give Anne a voice."

"I don't know…" Clara hesitated, picking at her mac and cheese. "I've never been involved in anything like that."

Ashlyn dabbed her mouth with a napkin. "You know, it will be more effective with many participants. Their energies can help bridge the realms. Do you have someone in mind? Your boyfriend, perhaps… what was his name?"

Clara's face darkened. "No, we broke up. It's just me here in Stowe. Well, mostly," she trailed off, a faint blush coloring her cheeks. "There is someone. Jack. We've become… friends. But I doubt he'd be into this sort of thing."

With a contemplative look, Ashlyn suggested, "Why don't we invite him?"

Clara hesitated, throwing Ashlyn a skeptical look. "Really? You think that's a good idea?"

In response, Ashlyn raised an eyebrow, her tone laced with dry amusement. "Would I suggest it if I didn't think it was a good idea?"

Despite the lingering doubt, Clara took a deep breath and dialed Jack's number, her fingers trembling as they hit the call button. She rehearsed her opening lines twice, attempting to smooth the nervous quiver in her voice. As the phone rang, anticipation knotted in her stomach. Then he picked up. His voice, deep and steady, resonated through the line, sending a fresh wave of uncertainty washing over her.

"Hey, Jack," she began, her voice shakier than she intended. "It's Clara. Remember when I told you about my consultant, Ashlyn Alden, for my last book?" She paused, trying to regain composure. "Well, she's here with me now. She believes a seance might help with my research for the novel, the one about Anne." Her words came out in a rushed stream, fueled by eagerness and apprehension. She swallowed hard, hoping her nerves weren't as transparent over the phone as they felt to her in that moment.

There was a pause, during which Clara looked at Ashlyn. "Look, I understand it's unorthodox, but if you're willing, it'd mean a lot to have you there. It's for the book, and maybe... to find some peace for Anne."

"Jack, you say?" Ashlyn's pendant, a crystal prism, caught the light as she leaned forward. "Would you mind if I spoke to him?"

Clara hesitated before nodding and handing it over to Ashlyn.

"Jack? This is Ashlyn Alden. Clara and I are planning a seance and she mentioned you. Would you be interested in joining? Your presence would be invaluable."

There was a pause, the muffled sound of Jack's voice emanating from the phone. Ashlyn's violet eyes sparkled with amusement. "Skeptics often make the best participants. Their grounded energy can be just what we need."

Another pause, longer this time, and then Ashlyn smiled, handing the phone back to Clara. "He'll join us."

After Jack's acquiescence, Clara let out a small laugh, relief flooding her system. "Thanks, Jack. I knew I could count on you. See you soon." She ended the call, her fingers lingering on the phone for a moment. Her heart raced, emotions churning inside. His willingness to step so far out of his comfort zone had to mean something, didn't it? Maybe he had a soft spot for her, even if it was just a tiny one

Ashlyn, picking up on Clara's mixed emotions, leaned in with a smile. "You're brave to embark on this journey. Something tells me it's not just about Anne or your book."

Clara's cheeks tinged pink. "Is it that transparent?"

"You have a certain... spark when you talk about Jack." Ashlyns eyes twinkled. "You like him, don't you?"

A soft sigh escaped Clara's lips. "That obvious, huh?"

Ashlyn chuckled. "To those who've been around the block a few times." She paused, scanning the cafe menu. "How about a glass of wine to calm those nerves?"

The offer made Clara pause. She wanted to be back in a better place. "Mmm, no thank you. I appreciate the offer. Maybe some chamomile tea instead?"

Lorelei's eyebrows raised. "Chamomile it is." She signaled the waiter, who nodded in acknowledgment and moved to fetch their order.

The two women spent the next half hour engrossed in a light conversation, discussing everything from the latest books they'd read to their mutual admiration for small New England towns. As the waiter returned with their drinks, Clara took a moment to savor the aroma of her tea, letting the warm, calming scent wrap around her.

Ashlyn watched, her eyes softening. "Sometimes the smallest choices are the most defining. Choosing chamomile today might seem insignificant, but it's a step in the right direction."

After settling the bill, Clara caught Ashlyn's eyes and felt a shiver run down her spine. They seemed to harbor secrets from ages past, their depth uncanny. Ashlyn's knack for grasping Clara's unspoken challenges was perplexing. How could she know?

Then, the realization washed over her like a wave. Of course—Ashlyn was psychic, but not the kind who read palms at carnivals. She had a gift. Clara recalled tales of Ashlyn's guidance, her ability to perceive what lay beyond the visible, tangible world.

A subtle smile played on Ashlyn's lips, almost as if she were reading Clara's thoughts right then, reinforcing

Clara's belief in her powers. Shaking her head, Clara was struck by the ways of the universe. "Thanks for getting it. I'm really hoping tonight clears things up, not just for Anne, but for me, too."

Ashlyn's nod carried wisdom. "Life has a way of weaving our paths with purpose. And remember, clarity often comes when we least expect it."

Rising from their seats, Clara felt a surge of confidence she hadn't possessed before.

As Ashlyn draped a lace shawl around her slender shoulders, the jewelry on her wrists glittered, capturing the sunlight streaming through the windows. They headed to the exit, side by side, the surrounding atmosphere charged with expectation.

After exchanging farewells, Clara wandered the streets of Stowe. Cobblestone pathways beneath her feet echoed with each step, a reminder of the town's history. She passed colonial-style buildings, each facade told a story, from ancient apothecaries to modern coffee shops. Baskets of vibrant flowers hung from lampposts, their petals swaying in the summer breeze.

Every corner seemed to hold a story or a secret, and for Clara, it served as the perfect distraction. She anchored herself in the present, pushing away the looming shadows of the upcoming seance.

Drawn to the inviting facade of a boutique, Clara stepped inside 'Lila's Closet.' The smell of fresh jasmine filled the air, mingling with the soft notes of a vintage record playing in the background. Clara browsed the curated selection of garments, admiring the material.

Then, the name of the store clicked in her mind. *Lila*. The connection was undeniable, given the size of Stowe. Clara's suspicions were confirmed as she locked eyes with a woman standing behind the counter.

It had to be her. Lila stood tall and graceful, her silhouette reminiscent of a delicate willow. Golden tresses flowed down her back, catching the ambient lighting.

Dressed in a silk blouse and high-waisted trousers, the woman moved with a confidence that dominated the surrounding space. Her presence was commanding, yet there was an underlying vulnerability in her posture.

Clara's heart twinged with insecurity, and she took a deep breath to find her ground. Lila radiated beauty and confidence, moving through her space with a grace that seemed almost daunting. Everything about her—the boutique, her aura, her effortless elegance—spoke of a self-assurance Clara found intimidating.

Her mind whirled, drawing comparisons and contrasts. Did Jack still have feelings for Lila? Were there remnants of emotion that could overshadow any connection Clara might build with him? It wasn't just about looks, either. It was the history the connections once shared that weighed on Clara.

A storm of doubt brewed inside her. How could she compare to Lila? These spiraling thoughts threatened to consume her, but Clara forced herself to breathe, to anchor in the moment. She was here for a purpose, not to drown in self-comparison. Yet, the seed of insecurity had taken root, and confronting it seemed inevitable.

Clara exhaled, attempting to steady her thoughts. She reminded herself that her daydreams of Jack, as vivid as they were, didn't signify something deep—it could just be a fleeting attraction. She was in Stowe for her book, not to find a relationship. Whatever was unfolding with Jack it shouldn't detract from her focus.

Closing her eyes, Clara conjured images of her Boston apartment, the city's skyline, her favorite coffee spot just around the corner—her life. A peace enveloped her. Jack was part of her Stowe experience, not the entirety of it.

With a refreshed resolve, Clara explored the boutique, setting aside the unsettling feelings and immersing herself in the moment. After all, finding beauty in the most unexpected places had always been her gift.

"Ah, you have an expert eye," Lila remarked as Clara picked up a vintage brooch, its design shimmering under the soft boutique lights.

"Thank you," Clara responded, her voice attempting a casual tone. "It reminds me of something my grandmother used to wear."

Lila leaned in, her green eyes assessing. "New to Stowe? I don't recall seeing you around."

"Just visiting," Clara admitted. "I am here for inspiration and research for my next book."

"A writer," Lila mused. "That's intriguing. I've always loved stories."

As Clara searched for her next words, Lila's voice dropped a shade cooler. "You know, stories can be deceiving. Just like people."

There was an undercurrent, a tension she hadn't expected. *Does she know?* She wondered. *That I know who she is? That I've been spending time with Jack?*

Lilas voice was dripping with insinuation. "Jack, for instance, is quite the raconteur, isn't he? He paints such vivid pictures with his words. Makes everyday occurrences seem almost... magical."

Clara felt a sting of unease, the pointedness of Lila's observation not lost on her. "Jack has been nothing but supportive since I got here. He's been a steady presence in an otherwise unfamiliar territory."

Lila's lips curled into a faint smirk. "All I'm saying is, be wary. People often showcase only the parts of their life that they're comfortable sharing."

The air between them grew tense. Clara revisited her interactions with Jack. Was Lila being spiteful, or had she missed something about Jack? Why was the woman pushing this so hard? Did she know something Clara didn't, or was this just some ploy to unnerve her?

"I hope Stowe gives you all the inspiration you need," Lila said.

Clara nodded. "Thank you. I believe it already has."

As Clara stepped out of Lila's Closet, she was blinded by the afternoon sun—like waking from a dream or a cautionary fable. The door chime's gentle ring behind her marked the end of a tumultuous visit.

The boutique's scented air clung to her, now feeling more like a burden than a perfume. Clara tried to shake it off. What just happened in there? Lila's parting words left a shadow of doubt about her fledgling connection with Jack. She massaged her temples and hoped to clear the haze of uncertainty. She reminded herself, not for the first time, that her purpose here was her book, not a dramatic love affair.

Walking on, the town soothed her—the quaint streets, the old-world charm of the buildings, the embrace of the natural surroundings. Yet, beneath Stowe's idyllic surface, Clara now perceived many layers. She filed away the day's events, to be revisited when she was ready to face them. For now, she sought refuge in the simpler joys, like ice cream. A respite from the tangled web of human connections.

A large table had been set up for the evening's seance. The room was dim, with only the soft glow of several ornate ivory candles illuminating the space. They flickered, casting shadows on the walls that seemed to play in time with the anticipatory energy in the room. The rich scent of sandalwood filled the air, mingling with the faint aroma of burning sage—Ashlyns's chosen blend to cleanse and protect the environment.

Ashlyn was a figure of focus and calm amidst the ambient energy. Her raven-black hair cascaded down her back, moving as she walked around the room, positioning cushions in a circle on the floor. Her delicate fingers traced patterns in the air, invoking unseen forces, her violet eyes intense and searching.

Next to the table in the corner stood her spiritual companion for the evening—Sebastian. His silver hair, short and coiffed, contrasted with his black suit. An air of flamboyance surrounded him, mirrored in the bold strokes of eyeliner stressing his expressive hazel eyes. He had a theatrical yet genuine air, someone who had embraced his spiritual gifts and wasn't afraid to show it.

"Darling, the energy in here is electric," Sebastian said, waving a hand. "Are we sure this isn't overkill?" He chuckled, revealing a row of white teeth.

Ashlyn smirked, her intense demeanor softening for a moment. "Full of opinions, aren't you, Seb? Just wait."

Sebastian approached the table, inspecting the array of crystals and trinkets. "Well, if there's one thing I've learned, it's to never doubt you," he mused.

Every detail of the room—from the circle of salt to the strategically placed crystals—was arranged, not just for effect, but with a genuine intent to connect with the beyond. As the preparations concluded, an energy of expectancy settled, readying for the souls and stories soon to unfold.

"Clara," Ashlyn began, her voice serene but purposeful, "for our seance to reach Anne, we need an object connected to her. Something that reverberates with her energy."

Clara's mind flashed to the locket. "The locket," she said. "It's on my nightstand."

Sebastian, with an intrigued look, responded, "Items with historical resonance, particularly those that have witnessed powerful emotion, can serve as powerful mediums to the spirit world."

Clara moved to her nightstand, drawing out the locket. It felt cold to the touch, its metalwork shimmering in the candlelight.

"I've felt its pull ever since I found it." Clara handed the locket to Ashlyn. "If Annes's spirit is tied to anything, it's this."

Ashlyn held the locket with a sense of reverence, feeling its weight and tracing the engraved patterns with her fingertips. "With this as our guide," she murmured, "we shall try to bridge the chasm separating us from Anne."

A knock at the front door announced Jack's entrance. The atmosphere, thick with incense and anticipation, seemed to shift with his assertive presence. He paused, taking in the myriad of candles, the intricate symbols, and the unfamiliar faces. His eyes settled on Clara, offering a reassuring nod, before shifting to Ashlyn and Sebastian.

"Quite the setup," he remarked, attempting to mask his unease. He then turned to Ashlyn, extending his hand in greeting. "Jack. I've heard a lot about you."

Ashlyn assessed him with a hint of amusement and accepted the handshake. "Ashlyn. Clara speaks highly of you." She gestured toward Sebastian, "And this is Sebastian, a dear friend and a guide on our spiritual journey tonight."

Sebastian, rising with an air of grace, greeted Jack with a soft, almost melodic voice, "Pleasure to meet you."

Jack offered a polite nod, his gaze still wandering around the room, trying to make sense of everything. To Clara, his attempt to navigate this unfamiliar territory made him seem more human, less the invulnerable figure she knew.

Yet, as Clara watched him, memories of her encounter with Lila clouded her thoughts. What had Lila meant with those veiled comments? Was there a side to Jack she was unaware of?

"I appreciate you coming, Jack," Clara said, her voice wavering.

Jack's eyes softened, meeting hers. "I said I would."

Ashlyn's voice began almost a whisper, its cadence rising and falling like a lullaby. "Spirit of the bridge, spirit of sorrow, Anne Wentworth, we call upon thee." The chant was repetitive, and with each iteration, her voice became firmer, more insistent.

Sebastian, eyes closed, his posture relaxed yet attentive, responded in kind, adding depth to the invocation. His voice melded with Ashlyn's, creating a duet of resonance that seemed to ripple through the very fabric of the room.

The atmosphere became denser. Clara felt a deep tug within her, like an old wound being reopened. She clutched Jack's hand tighter, seeking comfort from its reassuring warmth. The room seemed to pulsate, each throb echoing her mounting anxiety and anticipation.

Jack's thumb stroked Clara's hand, trying to offer solace, though his eyes, darting around the room, betrayed his own unease. His confident demeanor was now replaced by a subdued tension.

The aroma of the burning sage grew more potent, causing Clara's eyes to water. Her throat felt constricted, not from the scent, but from the rising emotions threatening to spill forth.

From the walls, or perhaps from a space beyond them, a soundless hum began, more of a feeling than an actual sound. The sensation snaked up Clara's spine, making her shiver. Jack looked down at her, his eyebrows furrowing with concern.

The locket, lying in the center, glowed, the metal gleaming with an intensity that drew Clara's gaze like a magnet. Soft chimes, their melody floating through the air like an ancient lullaby, accompanied its shimmer.

Ashlyn's chant persisted, her voice tinged with emotion. "Anne Wentworth, come forth. Share with us your story, your pain. We seek to understand, to bridge the divide."

The room's temperature plummeted. Each exhale produced puffs of frost, contrasting with the warmth of the summer night beyond the windows. A chilling draft enveloped them, making Clara pull closer to Jack, seeking his warmth. He responded by wrapping an arm around her, pulling her close, his own apprehension clear in his tightened grip.

A sudden, profound sadness weighed upon Clara's heart. She felt tears prickling at the back of her eyes, a cascade of emotions not her own.

Above the locket, a mist materialized, shaping into a recognizable form. Clara's heart thudded, knowing that they were on the verge of connecting with Anne's spirit.

Ashlyn's voice turned tender, almost caressing. "Anne, we are here with open hearts and open minds. Speak to us."

The waiting spirit of Anne Wentworth seemed to hover, hesitating on the precipice of communication. The seance had begun.

As the mist above the locket coalesced, Anne's form became more distinct. She wore flowing Victorian attire and had a mournful countenance. Her eyes, deep wells of sorrow, fixed upon Clara, while she displayed visible unease and perhaps even disdain when glancing at Jack.

Clara's heart raced, feeling an inexplicable kinship with the spirit before her. Their gazes locked, and in that silent exchange, she felt waves of shared experiences, heartaches, and deep, haunting regrets.

Anne's voice came through Ashlyn's mouth and carried an emotional weight that pressed down on everyone in the room. "Deception and betrayal. My heart was but a plaything to him," she said, casting a scornful look at Jack, as if he were a painful reminder of her past.

"I had loved with all my innocence," Anne continued, her voice shaky. "He promised to elope with me, to free me from the shackles of my life. But he left me, abandoned and shamed. I was ruined in the eyes of society, alone, knowing that my love had been a lie."

As Anne's tragic story unfolded, Clara felt a chill. The words, though belonging to another era, felt close to home. The promises of love, the impending heartbreak—Clara sensed that her own recent experiences resonated with Anne's tale.

Jack shifted, his gaze darting between Anne and Clara. He tightened his hold on Clara's hand, as if wanting to reassure her of his genuine feelings.

Sebastian, sensing the heightened tension, intervened. "We are here to listen and understand. We wish to aid in any way we can."

Anne's gaze returned to Clara, her eyes pleading. "Do not let history repeat itself, dear one. Protect your heart from hollow promises. I am bound to my regrets and sorrows. I do not wish the same fate upon you."

Clara felt tears streaming down her face, her emotions a tumultuous mix of sympathy for Anne's tormented past and the vulnerable rawness of her own recent experiences. "I...I understand," Clara answered, her voice shaking. "Thank you for your warning, for sharing your story."

Anne's form, which had wavered, regained its solidity for a moment. Her sad smile deepened with gratitude. "Remember my words. Trust your intuition."

Before she could fade again, Jack interjected, his voice desperate. "But what about the other side of the tale? Doesn't the man deserve to tell his side? History is always layered, filled with multiple perspectives."

Anne's form stiffened at the mention of the name. "Thomas," she spat, her spirit seething with palpable anger. The temperature in the room dropped. "He shattered my trust, toyed with my love, and then cast me aside like a discarded plaything. There's no redemption for such cruelty."

Jack, taken aback by her vehemence but undeterred, continued, "Every tale has two sides. Maybe he had his reasons, pains, and regrets, too."

Anne's form became threatening, her voice a chilling echo in the room. "Do not test me. My anguish is real. Do not dare diminish them with conjectures about him."

Ashlyn, sensing the escalating tension, stepped in, her voice firm yet soothing. "Enough! We are here to listen and to heal, not to instigate further unrest. Thank you, Anne, for sharing your pain and your message."

Anne's form disintegrated, her parting words lingering in the cold air. "Remember what I have said. Guard your heart."

"Why did you have to confront her like that?" Clara, unsettled, turned to Jack. "Tonight was supposed to be about uncovering Anne's story."

Jack looked into Clara's eyes, his expression earnest. "I just think... every story is seen differently depending on where you're standing." He paused. "Sometimes, we judge too quickly. I'm sorry if I messed anything up.."

Clara remembered how Jack had rescued her from the bar, free of judgment, filled instead with genuine care. A twinge of regret reminded her of her own insecurities.

"Let's just take a breather," Clara suggested. "It seems we both could use one."

As the seance wrapped up, Clara mulled over the tangle of unresolved feelings, the complex nature of love and judgment, and the myriad interpretations of truth.

In the soft glow of candlelight, doubt and uncertainty played across Jack's features. Ashlyn, halting her actions, caught his gaze. She moved to a small desk, scribbled something on a card, and offered it to Jack. "For those moments when words find their way."

Jack accepted the card, reading not just the message but also the intention behind it, and nodded in understanding.

Sebastian, approaching with a mischievous sparkle, teased, "For someone so grounded, you sure have a mysterious charm." He winked. "Or is it just your rugged good looks?"

A smile broke through Jack's contemplative mood. "Considering the source, I'll take that as a compliment."

Sebastian's laughter warmed the atmosphere. "Well played!"

As Ashlyn packed away her equipment, she observed, "Some nights leave a deeper imprint than others. Tonight's one of them."

Clara embraced Ashlyn, murmuring a heartfelt, "Thank you. Words just can't capture tonight."

"Sometimes, they don't have to," Ashlyn reassured her, patting her back.

Sebastian gave Clara an elaborate bow. "Till we meet again, dear Clara." He then turned to Jack, smirking, "And you keep dodging those spirits. The earthly ones, at least."

Jack's response came with a chuckle. "I'll do my best."

As the evening came to a close, Ashlyn and Sebastian's departure left Clara and Jack alone in the quiet aftermath.

The room, with its lingering traces of incense and spent candle wax, became a canvas for her reflections. Every shadowed corner seemed to hold a piece of Anne's tale, echoing with unresolved histories and pain.

Thoughts of Lila clouded Clara's thoughts, each one layered with uncertainty and an ever-growing sense of jealousy. Lila's vague comments, her cryptic insinuations, the glint in her eyes - it all made Clara's stomach churn with unease. Unbidden, an image of Jack and Lila together, arms and legs and cream-colored skin, making Clara's heart constrict, emotions threatening to overwhelm her.

Jack, rubbing the back of his neck, hesitated before speaking, "I don't know how much stock I put into... all of this." He gestured around the room. "But I can't deny what I saw, what we all experienced."

His words hung in the air, an attempt at understanding, at seeking common ground. Clara didn't respond, her gaze distant, lost in the maze of her own emotions.

He took a tentative step toward her, reaching out to touch her cheek to bridge the gulf that had opened between them. She flinched, pulling away from his hand. The walls she'd built, the defenses against hurt and betrayal, seemed more solid than ever.

"Clara…" Jack began, the pain of rejection in his voice.

But she cut him off, her voice a barely audible whisper. "I need time, Jack."

His eyes filled with confusion and a flicker of hurt. He searched her face for answers. For a moment, his jaw clenched, hinting at a suppressed anger or perhaps frustration. "I see…" he finally murmured, his voice colder than she had ever heard.

Without another word, he turned and made his way to the door. As it closed behind him, a tear trickled down Clara's cheek as regret overwhelmed her. She berated herself for allowing insecurities to overshadow her judgment, feeling both foolish and pained by the unexpected chasm that had formed.

CHAPTER SIX

A Love Rediscovered

The room felt cold and empty as Clara threw on a t-shirt and prepared for bed. Every noise seemed louder, every shadow deeper. Her conversation with Jack pressed down, filling her with regret. She toyed with calling him, to apologize, to explain, to just hear his voice. But what would she say? Maybe it was best to let things settle.

Her mind shifted to the bar. For a moment, she felt the familiar urge to go grab a drink and drown the maelstrom of feelings. That had gone poorly last time. She took a deep breath, reminding herself of the commitment she made earlier. Today *had* to be Day One.

Instead, Clara reached for the locket she had moved to the bedside table. She traced its carvings. The cool metal pulsed under her fingers, whispering secrets and stories.

As soon as her fingers made contact, a presence surrounded her: the haunting fragrance of roses filled the air, and a breeze rustled her curtains even though the window was shut. The world outside faded away as Clara lost herself in those tales that teased her senses and drew her deeper into Anne's memories and emotions.

In the secluded corners of Anne's world, Clara recognized the same desperate need to drown out the pain of reality. It wasn't alcohol for Anne, but the touch of a forbidden lover. There was a heady intoxication of sneaking glances and stolen kisses. Each era had its own form of escape, its own salves for the wounds of the heart and soul.

Anne's way of losing herself mirrored Clara's own struggles. Both women, separated by time, sought solace in something—or someone—that promised a brief respite from the pain. Just as Clara drowned her sorrows in a drink, Anne sought refuge in Thomas's embrace. Their love, though passionate, was also a dangerous diversion from the oppressive confines of her life.

As the memories flowed, Clara felt a strange kinship with Anne. They were both prisoners of their desires, struggling to find balance and control. They were women shaped by their times, by societal judgments, and by their own inner demons. It was a haunting realization: they were not so different. Tendrils of Anne's emotions wound their way around Clara, intertwining their yearnings and regrets. Past sins and the sweetness of forbidden pleasures fused with Clara's own heartbeat until she did not know which was her own and which where Anne's. She felt the unbridled rage at the fact that Thomas left her. Or was it Ethan? Jack would leave them both, too.

As morning came, Clara woke, her mind ablaze. The locket had shared its secrets, and she felt compelled to honor them. She would keep it near, drawing inspiration from its depths, and perhaps in doing so, offer Anne's spirit solace. The weight in her hand felt like more than just metal and stone. With each pulsation of its icy surface against her skin, she couldn't help but think of Anne and the suffocating world she was tethered to. A world where she had been constrained by the rigid bars of societal expectation.

In this age, Clara mused, Anne could've thrived, embracing her desires without the shame that once haunted her. An overwhelming sense of displacement swept over Clara, as if another presence sought to claim her. In a desperate bid to regain control, she hurled the locket across the room.

Feeling herself return, Clara grabbed her phone. Ashlyn would help. "The locket," she started, "I think it's trying to possess me!."

On the other end, sighed responded with a weighty sigh. "I was worried about that. It might be safer if I held onto it."

A sudden draft caused Clara's hair to dance around her face, and she could've sworn she felt the brush of fingertips on her wrist. A gentle yet desperate plea. She caught the flicker of a shadow, and its presence felt less threatening and more... imploring. She felt Anne's sadness, her loneliness and couldn't bring herself to dismiss the woman. Not yet.

"I...I'm not so sure I can give it up," Clara hesitated, the silent plea from the entity growing stronger, desperate. It seemed to beg her to hold on to the memories it safeguarded.

"Energies this powerful can be dangerous," Ashlyn warned over the phone. "If you're sure you want to keep it, be very careful." Clara could almost feel Ashlyn's worried gaze through the line.

She held the phone a little tighter and replied, "I know, I just... there's something about it. It feels important, like it's meant to be with me." She paused, considering Ashlyn's caution. "But I hear you. I'll be extra cautious, I promise."

The call ended, leaving Clara staring across the room at the locket. She picked it up, careful not to touch it for too long, and placed it on the edge of the desk where she wrote. Despite the warmth outside, an unyielding chill pervaded the room. Each keystroke echoed back to her, creating a duet with an unseen partner. The stories flowed not from her mind, but as if whispered directly into her.

The phone's chime broke the spell, causing her to jump. It was Jack. Clara's heart rate quickened, uncertainty making her fingers tremble over the device. Should she answer? Was he angry with her?

She took a deep breath and swiped to answer. "Hey," she began.

"Clara," Jack's voice came through, maintaining a careful lightness, "how about lunch?" Despite his attempt at casualness, Clara could detect strain, a concealed tension in his words.

She hesitated, a series of thoughts flashing through her mind. The morning's events, the ghostly whispers guiding her writing, the ever-present chill in her room despite the summer outside — it all swirled around her, creating a vortex of uncertainty.

"Clara?" Jack's voice cut through, bringing her back to the present.

She took a breath, feeling the locket's presence against her skin. "Yes, alright. Lunch sounds... nice," she finally responded, though the word seemed an inadequate description of the maelstrom of emotions she felt.

As Clara prepared to leave, the locket in her hand seemed to thrum with an unspoken yearning, almost as if urging her to take it along. Hesitating for a split second, she eventually placed it in her desk drawer, feeling an odd sense of parting. Dressed in a light summer dress, she began her short walk to the cafe to meet Jack, sensing a shift in the atmosphere with each step she took.

While she didn't know many in town by name, the stares were clear. The subtle pause in conversations, the slight turn of heads, and hushed tones made her aware of her surroundings. She took a deep breath, steeling herself as she approached the cafe. Somehow, she had become the other woman.

Jack stood outside, waiting. As she approached, their eyes locked—a silent understanding passing between them. They walked inside together, choosing a corner table. The atmosphere in the cafe was alive, but for them, the world seemed paused.

There was a long silence before Clara took a deep breath. "About last night... and the other night at the bar... I feel like there are things we haven't said, things I need you to know." She swallowed hard, avoiding direct eye contact. "I'm leaving in a few weeks, Jack. But it's more than that. After the bar incident, I started questioning how you see me. I don't want to be perceived as just... reckless."

She chanced a look at him, trying to gauge his reaction. "And I just got out of a relationship. Everything's still raw. I'm guarded, scared, and still figuring things out."

Jack's face remained inscrutable, though a muscle twitched in his jaw. "Clara," he began, his voice betraying his own vulnerability, "our time together has been... unexpected. But I'm not one to jump to conclusions or box someone into stereotypes. However, I do value clarity."

He paused, running a hand through his hair. "Look, I don't know what all this is. But I know I enjoy being around you. And if we only have a few weeks? I think it's worth making the most of it. Without... complications."

Clara frowned. "It's not about complications, Jack. It's about understanding. I don't want to mislead you, but I also don't want to regret not giving this—whatever this is—a chance."

Jack looked into her eyes, and for a moment, both of them allowed their defenses to drop. "Then let's take it one day at a time," he finally said. "No promises, no expectations. Just... us."

As they sat across from each other, the air was thick with tension. Clara took a deep breath and steadied herself. "There's something else," she started, her voice steady. "Ever since we first met, I've been getting these stares... and then bumping into Lila in town, her insinuations... I need to know the truth."

Jack winced, his eyes closing as if to shield himself from an unseen blow. When he looked up again, his features were set in a resigned expression. "It's complicated," he admitted. "After I left Stowe and went off to college, I started a new life in Providence. Lila and I had broken up. But then she appeared out of nowhere, and we gave it another go. For a while, everything seemed perfect."

Clara leaned back in her chair, listening.

He pressed on. "Lila dreamed of settling down in Stowe, closer to our roots. I chose her, my love for her overshadowing everything else. We made the move back, got married. But there was some resentment. I couldn't shake off the feeling that I had sacrificed my dreams for us."

"And then?" she urged.

Jack ran his fingers through his hair. "I won't lie to you, Clara. I struggled with anger. It was never directed at her, not in the way people think, but our home was filled with tension. Arguments became our new norm."

Clara saw a deep-seated regret. "And her...?"

With a whisper, Jack confessed, "She had an affair." His shoulders slumped. "When everything blew up, she didn't correct anyone. Just let the whole town spin a tale that made her out to be the victim, implying that it was my anger that pushed her away, into someone else's arms." Clara mulled over her thoughts, her mind replaying the conversation with Lila. "So, the town's convinced that..." she began, her voice trailing off as she sought the right words.

"That I was the aggressor," Jack cut in. "They think her infidelity was justified because of me. That I was a wife beater. But Clara, I swear, I never laid a hand on her."

There was an undeniable sadness in his eyes, a rawness that spoke volumes. Clara hesitated before she said, "In small towns, rumors have a way of becoming someone's unwanted reality. It's hard to know what's true."

He met her gaze, searching for belief. "Living under the shadow of these lies, feeling like you're constantly on trial—it's like you're gasping for air."

Clara felt a shift in the conversation was overdue. "Speaking of trials, last night's events... maybe we should look more into Thomas's actions, don't you think?"

Jack's features contorted. A fleeting look that was hard to decipher crossed his face before he could compose himself again. "Would seem even ghosts struggle with rumors."

They were slowly becoming the center of attention. "Maybe we should continue this somewhere less public?" Clara suggested.

He nodded. "There's a quiet spot by the lake. Away from the gossip."

With a cautious smile, Clara replied, "Let's go."

As they left the cafe, the cool air wrapped around them. Jack led the way through the town's winding streets, greeting a few familiar faces with a nod or a wave, but never stopping to chat. Now and then, he'd glance over at Clara, as if checking she was still there beside him.

They soon reached the edge of town, where the asphalt gave way to a dirt path lined with tall pine trees on either side. "It's just a bit further," Jack said.

The trees opened up to reveal a breathtaking view. They stood atop a hill overlooking a serene lake, its surface a mirror reflecting the soft pastel hues of the setting sun. Nearby, a lone bench sat facing the water, inviting them to rest.

"This is my sanctuary," Jack said, more to himself than to Clara. "Whenever the world becomes too much, I come here to clear my head."

They took a seat, and for a while, they just sat in silence, soaking in the natural beauty around them. The gentle lapping of the water against the shore, the distant call of a bird, Jack's hand as it brushed against Clara's—all of it painted a picture of peace.

"I can see why you love it here," Clara murmured.

He turned to her, their faces inches apart. "It's even better with company."

Their eyes locked, and something passed between them. The sorrow and understanding, the hope for a new beginning, the undeniable chemistry that had been building since their first meeting. There was a silent beckoning that neither could ignore. Her world fell away as Jack's gaze dropped. Time seemed to stretch as he hesitated for a heartbeat.

Their lips with a tenderness that caught them both off guard. As they leaned into each other, the soft caress deepened, pulling them into a vortex of emotions they had been skirting around.

When they finally pulled away, their breaths mingled in the cooling evening air. Clara felt a flutter in her chest, her heart trying to match rhythm with the emotions coursing through her.

Then the realization struck her like a bolt of lightning. Their relationship was living on borrowed time. Clara hadn't come to this town with intentions of permanence. Her visit was a brief interlude, a space for healing, creativity, and perhaps a dash of excitement. She never expected forging a bond, especially one with as complicated a history as Jack's.

She tried to shake off the thought, but it clung to her, the weight pressing on her chest. "Jack," she began, looking up at him, "what are we doing?"

He frowned, sensing her sudden shift. "What do you mean?"

"This," she gestured between them, "Us. I won't be here forever. I came here to escape, to write, and... and then I met you. And it's been wonderful, but..."

Jack placed a gentle finger on her lips, silencing her. "Clara, I know," he whispered. "Believe me, I've thought about it too. But didn't we agree to take this one day at a time? Can't you just be in the now?" He paused, his eyes searching hers. "Tomorrow is uncertain for everyone. What matters is this moment, and right now, I want to be with you."

Clara met his gaze, and a pang of hurt washed over her. Her need for reassurance about their future seemed dismissed by his plea for the present.

Clara looked out at the horizon. Could she even separate the present from the past and future? It was a dance she hadn't quite mastered, even in past relationships. Could she indulge in the now, in the connection she felt with Jack, without binding her heart to the future's uncertainties? Was it even fair to Jack or herself to attempt such a balance? It all made her head spin.

She took a deep breath, the crisp air filling her lungs, and turned to Jack. "I think I should go home," she murmured. "I need some time to think, to figure things out."

Jack's brows furrowed as a shadow of disappointment passed over his face. Yet, his expression softened almost immediately. He took a step closer, bridging the distance between them. "Alright," he whispered. Then, tilting her chin up, he pressed his lips to hers. It wasn't a long kiss, but one full of promise. As he pulled away, Clara was left breathless, even more conflicted than before.

When she returned to the cabin, Clara sensed an immediate change. The air was thick with a kind of melancholy, an intangible sadness that filled the space. Soft, sorrowful sobs seemed to drift through the rooms, serving as a constant reminder of the unseen presence dwelling alongside her. Now and then, a brief glimpse of white—a ghostly figure of a woman in a flowing dress—would appear just out of sight, disappearing the moment Clara tried to focus on it.

The occasional touch of cold, ghostly fingers against her skin still made Clara shiver, but the tremors were now mixed with a budding familiarity. Shadows around her seemed to pulse with unspoken emotions. "Living with a ghost mourning its own loss is more difficult than I ever imagined," Clara murmured to herself, feeling an odd sense of connection growing within her.

As she sought to narrow the distance between her world and the spectral realm, Clara reached for Anne's locket and clasped it. She lay down, the icy touch against her chest no longer felt cold but somehow grounding. It acted as a conduit to Anne's spirit, steadying Clara as she slipped into a trance, her senses intertwining with the ghost's sorrows.

The experience was far from serene. As soon as she closed her eyes, Clara found herself immersed in a sea of memories that weren't her own. She was transported to the barn, which, contrary to its usual mysterious shadows in her dreams, was now bathed in sunlight. The light seeped through the wooden slats, casting speckled shadows on the hay-strewn floor.

In this scene, Anne and Thomas were wrapped in an intimate embrace. Clara could almost touch the passion that radiated between them. The barn was their sanctuary, a place for tender moments, their love deepening with every furtive look and touch that lingered longer than it should.

But as the dreamscape continued to shift, Clara was outside the barn, under a vast expanse of inky sky speckled with stars. Thomas, with a nervous determination in his eyes, knelt before Anne, presenting a small box. As he opened it, the glint of a delicate ring caught the moonlight, the promise it held shining brighter than any jewel. The joy in Anne's eyes, the tears glistening on her cheeks, and the embrace they shared filled Clara's heart with warmth. The dreamscape encapsulated the purity and hope of their love — a life they dreamed of building together.

But dreams and memories are often unpredictable. The radiant landscape darkened, shifting to a scene of desolation. Anne stood at the bridge, her wedding dress flowing in the night breeze. She looked at the path, anticipation clear in her eyes. A small lantern by her side cast eerie shadows, flickering and revealing her face contorted with concern, then sadness. The hours seemed to stretch, and yet Thomas was nowhere in sight.

As midnight came and went, Anne's hope dwindled, replaced by the heartbreak of a love interrupted, promises unfulfilled. Clara awoke with a jolt, feeling the remnants of Anne's emotions—the soaring joy and the crushing despair—echoing in her own heart.

Clara had seen the love in Thomas' eyes. Something was wrong. Jack's intuition to hear the other side of the tale had been right. It was imperative they unearthed the reasons for Thomas's no-show. They owed it to Anne and Thomas, and maybe, in some strange way, they owed it to themselves. Restlessness consumed her, an urge that pulsed with every heartbeat, growing louder and impossible to ignore.

She placed the locket on the coffee table, its metallic surface catching the faint moonlight streaming through the window, and scrambled off the couch. As the cool night air kissed her skin, she moved instinctively, her thoughts a blur of urgency. Without realizing what she was doing, she had grabbed a hoodie, pulling it over her head, and slipped into her shoes. Every fiber of her being pulsated with a singular focus.

Compelled by this unshakable feeling, Clara began a frenzied search through the cabin. She rummaged through drawers, flipped through pages of books, and sifted through the small pile of receipts that had accumulated in the corner of the kitchen counter. Her hands moved of their own accord, driven by desperation. Then, amidst a stack of random paper, her fingers brushed against a small, unassuming card. There, in Jack's unmistakable handwriting, was an address.

She found herself in her car, the engine purring beneath the dashboard. The emotions, tangled and confusing, pressed on her chest. She needed clarity, an anchor amidst the emotional storm. Jack was that anchor. When she arrived at his place, she mustered her courage and knocked.

The door opened to reveal Jack's concerned gaze. "Clara? What are you—"

"I just needed to see you," she whispered.

He moved aside, letting her into the house. As she stepped through the entry, Jack closed the door behind her. Without a word, she leaned in. He backed away, his hands holding her shoulders.

"Clara, wait," he said. "You were the one that needed time to think."

Her hand touched his cheek. The air between them was filled with an awkwardness, a dance of emotions they hadn't quite learned the steps to.

"I'm sorry... I'm a mess," Clara said, her voice trailing off.

Jack smiled and replied, "It's okay, Clara. We're in a complicated spot, aren't we?"

There was a brief pause as they both considered their situation. The connection they shared was undeniable, but they were navigating a maze without a map.

Clara nodded. "Yeah, we are. I just... I guess I got carried away by the moment."

Jack's expression softened. "I understand. It's easy to do."

He led Clara into the living room, their footsteps quiet on the carpeted floor. They settled into the comfort of the couch, embarking on a journey through conversation. It spanned the mystery of Thomas' fate to the lighter moments that make life sweet. Laughter came easily, blending with more serious discussions. The night wrapped them in its embrace, passaging time marked only by the changing tones of their dialogue and the softening light.

Without realizing it, Clara's eyelids had grown heavy, the gentle cadence of their conversation weaving a lullaby that eased her into a deep, dreamless sleep. She awoke to the soft light of morning. The room was bathed in still-ness, save for the comforting aroma of coffee brewing in the distance. A blanket lay over her, which she pushed aside as she sat up, startled. What had happened?

Jack appeared at the doorway, a grin on his face. "Good morning, sleepyhead."

Clara blinked, confusion clear in her eyes. "I... what?"

"Don't worry," he chuckled. "You just fell asleep. Nothing happened."

Relieved that she hadn't embarrassingly overindulged, Clara accepted the coffee he offered.

"Up for a hike today?" he asked, his smile inviting.

Still disoriented, Clara simply nodded.

Before long, Clara and Jack ascended a trail leading to a vantage point overlooking Stowe.

"You come up here yet?" Jack asked, breaking the silence.

"No," Clara responded. "It's breathtaking."

"That's the thing about Stowe. Everyone knows the town, but not everyone sees its true essence," he remarked, leading her to a venerable maple tree. Then, unexpectedly, he pulled out a small sketchbook and captured her silhouette in pencil.

"You draw more than engineering stuff?" Clara asked, eyes wide.

He just gave her a wink.

She couldn't help but smile back. "You're full of surprises, Jack Thompson." In the week that followed, Clara and Jack grew closer, even though the past continued to cast a long shadow over them. One chilly evening, as a sudden draft swept through the cabin's living room, the flicker of candle flames was accompanied by a soft sob.

Jack's expression shifted to alarm as he felt an unexpected sting on his back. He turned, questioning, "Did you...?"

With wide eyes, Clara shook her head in denial. The light revealed three fresh, red scratch marks on his skin. "She's... she's letting us know she's here," Clara said.

Jack swallowed. "Maybe, for now, we should spend time together at my place. I don't think your ghost likes me very much."

Clara agreed. She had grown accustomed to Anne's presence, but the woman clearly didn't like Jack.

The following morning found them poring over a microfiche machine in the local library. Clara's fingers flew over the controls, sifting through historical records until a headline snagged her attention. "Here," she breathed out.

"Mysterious Disappearance Shocks Stowe: Local Gentleman, Missing." They leaned closer, devouring the words, only to find the story was about another man, lost decades after Anne's death.

Disappointment settled on Clara. "It's not him," she murmured.

Jack's arm found its way around her waist. "We won't give up. We'll find what we're looking for," he assured her.

Their research was interrupted by Clara's phone. "Ashlyn?" she said, puzzled, putting the call on speaker. "You are on speaker with Jack and me."

Ashlyn's voice flowed through, light and full of purpose. "Perfect timing, then. I'm glad Jack is with you. You will both want to hear this. Jack, something you said during our session the other day struck a chord with me. I often guide the living, but your insight reminded me of our responsibility to the departed, ensuring they find peace."

Jack nodded in agreement, touched by the sentiment.

Ashlyn continued, "I spoke with someone familiar with local lore and Thomas's lineage. They've uncovered family journals, amongst other things that might shed light on that fateful night."

Clara's heart leapt. "What did you find?"

"It's too much for a call. Can we meet?" Ashlyn proposed.

Clara and Jack exchanged a glance, a silent agreement passing between them. "Jack's place would be best," Clara suggested. "My rental seems to be…occupied by Anne's spirit. Particularly around the locket. I'll text you the address."

"See you then," Ashlyn confirmed

The two of them walked to the parking lot together. Jack turned to Clara, his eyes searching hers. "You could…stay the night."

Clara felt a familiar heat rise in her. The temptation was undeniable, but she also felt the pull of her writer's obligation. She placed a hand on his cheek. "I need to get some writing done, Jack. But I promise I'll see you tomorrow."

He nodded, respecting her decision. They shared a lingering gaze before parting ways. That evening, Clara settled by the window, cradling the locket in her palm. The intricate designs felt cold against her skin, a direct contrast to the fervent emotions they encapsulated. The passionate love that Anne held for Thomas mirrored her own feelings for Jack.

A chill seemed to seep into the room. The locket, responding in kind, shimmered with a muted glow. Thoughts of her imminent departure from Stowe crowded her mind. While she looked forward to returning to her apartment in Boston, the thought was bittersweet. All traces of Ethan would be gone. She'd return to an emptiness, both in the apartment and in her heart, but it would be a fresh start.

She reached for her journal and wrote, letting her emotions flow. Every experience with Jack, every stolen moment, and their intense connection poured onto the pages. Amidst her scribbles, a few lines formed a spontaneous verse:

In Stowe's dark heart, I kindled a fire,
With you, Jack, my secret desire.
Yet we might break worlds, pulling us apart.
But your shadow, forever, haunts my heart.

Despite her deep yearning, Clara knew Stowe was just a detour in her life's journey. The energy of the city awaited her, though the thought of leaving Jack behind gnawed at her soul.

The room's chilliness retreated, replaced by a comforting warmth. It felt like a protective embrace, and Clara knew it was Anne. There was a sense of gratitude in the air, a silent thank you for shining a light on a story that had been shrouded in darkness for so long.

CHAPTER SEVEN

Old Flames

Clara's morning in town was filled with errands, culminating in a visit to the coffee shop for a well-deserved treat. As she lined up to order, she felt the atmosphere shift. Two older women, deep in conversation at a nearby table, shot Clara a look that was as quick as it was guilty. Then, their voices dropped to a whisper. Despite every instinct telling her she was the subject of their hushed tones, Clara attempted to focus on the pastries in front of her.

"…you know what he did last summer?" one of them whispered.

"Should we warn her?" the other muttered, her voice laden with concern.

The incessant whispering sent Clara's heart pounding. As someone who cherished her anonymity, she was outraged to suddenly become the subject of local gossip. Trying to keep her anger in check proved futile as she ordered a muffin and a small black coffee. When she caught another glimpse of the women, she saw not just pity but condescension in their eyes before they looked away. Fury surged through her. "If you have something to say, then have the guts to say it to my face!" she snapped as she stormed out of the store, slamming the door behind her.

As Clara walked down the street, she felt the pervasive gaze of the town's judgment, yet there was a part of her that hesitated. She questioned if perhaps there was a place for her in this small town. The community's warmth, though often overshadowed with scrutiny, hinted at a genuine connection. Jack, with his earnest efforts, was chipping away at her resolve. But the thought of returning to Boston lingered in her mind. It was and always would be home.

Back at her cabin, Clara unpacked her groceries, eager to write. A knock interrupted her solitude. She flung open the door to find Lila standing there, her hair perfectly styled and an unbearable air of sophistication around her. Clara felt an immediate and intense surge of dislike. This day had gone from bad to worse.

"Hello Clara." Lila's voice was soft with condescension.

Swallowing the lump in her throat, Clara respond-ed, "Can I help you?"

Lila extended her hand. "We met at my store, but I felt a formal introduction was in order. I'm Lila." she began, her tone layered.

As Lila's eyes flitted past Clara's shoulder, Clara couldn't help but interject, "If you're wondering, Jack's not here." Lila's lips curled into a smirk.

Outside, the faint rustling of leaves provided a sound-track to the awkward silence that filled the room. Clara's heart raced, sensing the storm brewing between them.

"Why are you here?" Clara felt no need for niceties.

"You seem to have made quite an impression on our little town," Lila began.

Clara straightened, refusing to let Lila's presence intim-idate her. "Stowe has its charm. I've found reasons to like it here."

Lila's lips twitched. "And some of those reasons have dark hair and piercing eyes, I presume?"

Choosing her words, Clara replied, "Jack and I... We've become friends."

"Friends?" Lila chuckled, her laughter devoid mirth. "It's just... Jack and I have history, Clara. Deep, long history. You might be the talk of the town now, but you'll move on, and he'll be left behind, hurt."

Clara squinted her eyes. Was this woman trying to protect him? "Jack is a grown man. We know what we're getting into. And you don't get to dictate how he feels or who he spends time with."

"You're just a passing phase, a novelty." Lila's eyes flashed. "Once the thrill fades, where will that leave you? Do you think you are the first tourist he has fallen for?"

This was getting stranger by the minute., Now it seemed like this woman was trying to protect her. Maybe Lila was just crazy.

"I'm not here for games," Inside, Clara's heart twinged. But on the surface, she held strong. "What Jack and I have might be short-lived, but it's genuine and none of your business."

For a moment, Lila looked taken aback by Clara's boldness. Then, with a sigh, Lila relented. "Just remember, everything in this town has consequences. Jack's already been through a lot."

Clara's eyes softened. "I don't want to hurt him. But I also won't be scared off by town gossip or veiled threats. I'm here for the rest of this week, and I'm going back to Boston. Until then, how Jack and I choose to spend our time is our business."

Lila studied Clara for a heartbeat longer, then nodded. "Very well. Just... be careful."

With that, Lila turned and left, leaving Clara full of confusion. As the door closed, Clara's facade of strength wavered. *I'm not here for long... Do I need this small-town drama?* Shaking her head, Clara reminded herself to focus on the present and let the future take its course.

In the quiet of her rental, Clara watched as shadows lengthened around her, mirroring her thoughts. Lila's warning echoed in her mind, stirring a tension she couldn't dismiss. Did Jack's history with tourists matter? Clara considered herself far from perfect.

Her footsteps creaked on the wooden floorboards as she walked to the small table and rested her fingers on Anne's locket. Its chill sent a shiver through her, sparking feelings of anger, an emotion Anne must have known well. The locket encapsuled Anne's feelings about trust and love, particularly towards men.

Yet Clara knew her situation with Jack differed from Anne's tale. Theirs was a fleeting connection, not a doomed romance. However, But the thought of Jack's warm touch and his soft whispers left Clara torn. She needed to process her encounter with Lila, especially with her meeting Ashlyn at Jack's coming soon.

How would Jack react to hearing about Lila's confrontation? Would he be defensive? Concerned? Or dismissive? The more she thought about it, the more conflicted she felt. Part of her sought reassurance, but another part, influenced by Anne's spirit, nudged her towards self-preservation. She felt a strong need to divorce herself from this situation. Lila clearly still had some sort of feelings for Jack. Did he return them?

As the day progressed, Clara tried to shake off her doubts. As she prepared to meet Ashlyn, she questioned whether she was ignoring the potential red flags. She touched the locket once more and wondered if she was being blindly hopeful. With a heavy heart, she left for Jack's, the unresolved feelings and Anne's locket lingering in her mind.

At Jack's place, the scent of brewing tea greeted Clara. Ashlyn was already settled in the living room, a small box cradled in her lap.

She stood in greeting, her voice soft and knowing. "I've brought something I think might help. Or at least, it's another piece to our puzzle."

Upon opening the box, Clara was greeted by the sight of a plain ring. It featured a band, devoid of any stones, reflecting Thomas's humble means. The ring's beauty lay in its minimalism, telling a story of genuine commitment beyond material wealth.

"Are you proposing?" Clara giggled. Ashlyns lips curled into a small smile.

"If I thought you would say yes..." she joked. "It belonged to Thomas' family. They have passed it down through generations. And, like your locket, this ring has its own spirit attached."

Clara shifted, "Haunted?"

Ashlyn nodded. "Haunted, but intelligently so. Unlike residual hauntings where you might witness a repeated action or hear the same sounds over and over, like a tape stuck on replay, intelligent hauntings involve spirits that are aware. They can interact, respond, even show emotions. This ring... it knows."

Clara frowned, trying to process what this meant. Another haunted artifact added yet another layer to the mystery of the day Anne died.

"Why do you think it's connected to our situation?" Jack inquired, his brow furrowed.

Ashlyn met his gaze. "From what my contacts have relayed, this was the ring Thomas gave to Anne. It was found in his belongings when he passed. The restless energy suggests it's waiting for something... or someone."

Clara reached out to touch the ring. A distinct sensation washed over her. The metal felt cool against her skin, and she could feel the stories from the past.

"We're going to use a spirit box," Ashlyn began pulling out a small electronic device from her bag. She had explained its purpose to Clara when they first met: a tool designed to scan radio frequencies, capturing fragments of sound that spirits could manipulate to communicate. Clara glanced at Jack, aware that the paranormal wasn't exactly his cup of tea. He shrugged. The living room was dim, the heavy curtains blocking out the early evening light. Ashlyn set the stage, placing candles in a circle on the coffee table and lighting them one by one. The flames flickered, casting shadows on the walls.

Clara eyed the device, her heart racing. The idea of contacting Thomas was exciting. Another side to the story. She remembered Anne's turbulent emotions during the seance. Would this be similar? If they could reach out to Thomas, perhaps they could piece together the entire story and help the spirits find peace.

"I'm ready," Clara said.

Jack's fingers drummed a steady rhythm on the armrest, his eyes flitting from the spirit box to Clara and back again. Even after all the strange events they'd encountered together, a shadow of skepticism hung over him.

Ashlyn caught the hesitation in Jack's demeanor and addressed it directly. "Jack," she began, drawing his gaze with her measured tone, "it's not about embracing every aspect of the paranormal. It's about opening a channel for Thomas to communicate." Jack paused, then nodded. A concession to the possibility.

As the spirit box cycled through frequencies, creating a static filled with snippets of sound, Clara and Jack shared a look. Clara could feel Jack's reservations lingering. She moved closer and offered him the ring. "Maybe it'll work better if you're the one holding it," she suggested. "Thomas might find it easier to connect with you."

Once Ashlyn paused the device, Jack grasped the ring, closing his hand around it. With the spirit box restarted, a static hum punctuated the room's silence.

"Focus on Thomas," she urged. "Remember his love for Anne. Let's bridge the years and hear what he's been longing to say."

Ashlyn adjusted the scan rate, ensuring that the white noise wasn't fast nor slow. The rhythmic shuffle of radio waves filled the room — snippets of songs, fragments of conversations, and static all merged into one continuous drone.

A few minutes in, amidst the white noise, a discernible pattern emerged — faint, but unmistakable. It was as if the white noise was punctuated by soft, drawn-out whispers.

"I... loved..." The voice was distant and static-laden, but there was an unmistakable emotion behind it.

Clara's heart raced, her eyes widening as she looked at Jack, who clutched the ring.

"...Anne..." the voice continued. Every time the name was mentioned, the electromagnetic sensor on the spirit box flickered, showing heightened activity.

"Thomas?" Ashlyn asked.

The answer came, not in words, but in an emotional surge through the radio waves, as though someone was trying to convey feelings more than specific messages. But among the feelings, two words were discernible, "...Held... back..."

Jack's grip on the ring intensified, as if trying to draw more from it. "What happened, Thomas? Why didn't you come?" He asked.

Amid the static and fleeting snatches of radio broadcasts, a clearer, more poignant message formed: "...Family... Anne's... Trapped..."

The trio sat in anticipation of more, only to be met with white noise. After they were sure Thomas had nothing more to say, Ashlyn retrieved some notes. "The family refused to release the old journals and documents, yet I discovered a journal detailing Thomas's confinement in a basement on the night he planned to elope with Anne. Anne's older brother uncovered their scheme, prompting the family to intervene."

"Did they know about the child?"

Ashlyn raised an eyebrow. "Child?"

"I... felt a connection to the locket and saw something ..."

With a sigh, Ashlyn replied, "There's no record of a child anywhere. It's probable that Thomas was unaware himself."

"Why didn't you mention these journals earlier?" Jack asked.

"I wanted to avoid influencing our expectations of the spirit box responses," she explained. "Sometimes, our desires can shape the messages we receive from the spirits."

Tears formed in Clara's eyes as a painful realization dawned on her. Thomas had never abandoned Anne, and she died for nothing. He had been trapped by the very people she called family. The tragic nature of their love story, tangled in misunderstandings and outside interference, struck a chord. Jack's living room walls seemed to close in on Clara. Thomas's love for Anne had been pure, yet the constraints of societal expectations and family honor had torn them apart.

She drew unsettling parallels between their ill-fated romance and the gossipy nature of Stowe. She realized that, though centuries had passed, the underlying human tendencies had changed little. Families then, like the whispering townsfolk now, felt an intense pressure to maintain a facade of respectability. The malicious whispers she had encountered earlier in the day seemed trivial compared to the actions of Anne's family, yet the essence was the same. Both then and now, people were quick to judge, to stifle, and to manipulate in the name of societal standing.

It made Clara wonder about the true nature of human progress. Had society evolved? Or were we all just echoes of the past, doomed to repeat the same patterns, just with different faces and stories? The thought was haunting, and Clara felt a shiver run down her spine.

Clara felt the emotions running high. Each of them seemed lost in their own thoughts. As she looked up, she noticed a subtle change in Jack's demeanor. The man who had started off this journey as a skeptic, doubting the supernatural, was now affected. There was a spark of excitement, a light of belief in his eyes that hadn't been there before.

"It's heartbreaking," Clara said, "how society can twist the course of true love. The cruel lengths Anne's family went to, just to uphold their reputation. It mirrors the gossipy vibes of Stowe, even now."

Jack nodded, brushing his fingers over the ancient ring. "Their love story deserves closure. They deserve to be together."

Ashlyn met Clara's eyes, then shifted to Jack. "This bond between Anne and Thomas is still strong. The ring and locket need to be united. And where better than the bridge? It was their chosen rendezvous point."

A realization dawned on Clara. "Tomorrow's June 13th, the anniversary of the day Anne died," she murmured.

"The night they were supposed to get married." Recognition flared in Jack's eyes, and his initial skepticism seemed like a distant memory.

"It's more than just a date. We have a unique opportunity here." Ashlyn added, "The universe has its mysterious ways, and maybe it's led us to this moment."

Clara's spirits lifted. "Tomorrow night, then. We'll reunite them at the bridge, giving them the peace and union they were denied in life."

After Ashlyn agreed and headed home for the night, Jack and Clara shared a moment of closeness. She could feel the steady beat of his heart against hers, its rhythm a comforting anchor in the surrounding tumult. He pulled her closer, and in that embrace, the chaos of the world seemed to fade away. His touch, gentle and protective, promised to keep her safe. Clara's heart, though full, carried a tinge of sadness. She cherished the warmth of Jack's body against hers, the protective circle of his arms, but knew that these moments were fleeting. They were caught at the crossroads of past and future.

"You're distant," Jack spoke in her ear. His breath against her neck sent shivers down her spine, but the weight in her heart remained.

After taking a shaky breath, Clara's voice wavered. "I leave in two days." The raw pain in her words was an unmasked wound, exposed to the world, aching with the cruelty of fleeting moments and imminent goodbyes.

Jack's fingers brushed a stray lock of hair behind her ear, his touch lingering on her skin, cool against the warm flush of her cheeks. His eyes searched her face as if trying to commit every detail to memory. "I know," he murmured, his voice tinged with the same melancholy that shaded her own. "Time has never felt so cruel."

He cupped her face, his thumbs tracing her cheekbones. "These days with you, Clara, have been more real than entire years of my life. It's like I've been sleepwalking until now."

Clara swallowed hard, the lump in her throat stubborn and painful. "But what happens when I go back to Boston? When this...whatever this is... becomes just a memory? Another story in a life full of them? Will you come see me?"

Jack's gaze didn't waver. "Memories fade, but feelings? They stay. Even if time and distance try to dilute them, some remain forever." He sighed. "I won't pretend to know the future, but I know this—what we have isn't ordinary. It's something you remember, no matter where life takes you."

Their foreheads touched, an acknowledgment of the feelings that tied them together. It was the pain of impending separation, but also the beauty of having experienced something worth cherishing.

Clara's eyes dropped to the floor, gathering her thoughts. Lila's visit, her words and implied threats, pressed down on her. Honesty, she believed, was the only way forward, especially given their time-bound relationship.

She looked up into Jack's eyes. "Jack... Lila came to see me today."

His expression changed, surprise flaring before settling into something more complex. "She did?" his voice was tense.

She nodded, swallowing. "Lila had... things to say about you two, about your past. I think she was trying to warn me off, maybe out of jealousy or perhaps genuine concern. I don't know."

His fingers tensed around her, then relaxed. "Lila and I... our history is long and complicated. It was intense, passionate, but also volatile. We loved hard, and we fought harder. But that's all in the past." He steeled himself. "I won't deny that there was love between us. But we've both changed. We grew apart. What we had is over."

Clara nodded, absorbing his words. "I figured as much. And honestly, what I felt today wasn't jealousy, but more... sadness. I'm sad because our time is limited, and it seems like shadows from the past loom larger than they should. What we have feels special. And I don't want it to be overshadowed by drama."

Jack smiled, brushing a thumb across her lips. "Then let's not let it be. We can't change the past or predict the future, but we have now. Let's cherish it."

But as they clung to each other, the shadows of Anne and Thomas's story loomed, a haunting reminder of love lost and destinies changed. Clara looked out of the window, the silhouettes of trees stark against the evening sky, their branches swaying like restless spirits.

Her thoughts drifted to Boston, a life waiting for her return, now cleared of remnants of a failed relationship. But Stowe had gifted her a story, an intense connection, and a dilemma. As the night deepened, Clara wondered if, like Anne, she too was on the precipice of a bittersweet chapter in her life.

CHAPTER EIGHT

Confronting the Past

As the mid-morning sunlight crept through the curtains, Clara awoke alone. The imprint where Jack had been lay empty. Was he already up, perhaps making breakfast? The lack of coffee smell said otherwise.

She sat up, her thoughts a tangle of confusion. As memories of the night before flooded her, she smiled, thinking of how they had made plans for him to spend the following evening at her rental. Tomorrow would mark her last night in Stowe, and after their mission of reuniting Anne and Thomas, they both wanted to spend her last night in town together, holding onto the magic just a little while longer.

She slid the soft sheets away and pivoted towards the bedside table, where her eyes caught sight of a note. It rested there, its edges crumpled—evidence of Jack's haste. With a sigh of distaste for the all-too-familiar paper messenger, her fingertips grazed the note, unfolding it to reveal the message he had left.

Clara,

I hate to leave without saying goodbye, but something came up at the NYC office. They needed me there. It's complicated, but I promise it couldn't be avoided. Know that leaving you this morning was the last thing I wanted to do.

Once we're done at the bridge tonight, let's make some time for us — I owe you a night you won't forget, before you head back to Boston.

Jack

After reading the note, Clara's anger flared as she crumpled it in her hands. The warning bells echoed in her mind. She exhaled, allowing the note to fall onto the table. His abrupt departure and the promises in the note stirred a whirlwind of feelings. Anger bubbled up to the top, yet a flicker of hope persisted. They still had tonight. Clara's ride back to her rental was silent. The streets of Stowe seemed aloof and unyielding. The corners and landmarks that had once held the thrill of discovery together felt empty without Jack. She pulled into the driveway and shut off the engine. The quiet within the car echoed her own sense of solitude.

After lingering for a moment, she retrieved her phone.

A few agonizing seconds later, "Hey Clara," came Jack's familiar voice.

"I got your note," she began, striving for a calm tone, though her emotions threatened to spill over.

"Sorry Clara," Jack's voice crackled over the phone, the ambient noise of the city filtering through. "I didn't see this coming. They needed me."

"You mentioned that." She took a sharp inhale. "Jack, today was going to be ours."

"I know, I know. It's...complicated," he replied. "Look, once I'm done here, I promise to drive straight back. Even if it means flooring it the entire way."

Clara's voice trembled. "But will you make it by midnight?"

"I'll do everything in my power to be there. You have my word."

There was a brief silence, both grasping for the right words. Finally, Jack ventured, "You know, I could visit you in Boston."

Clara felt her walls rising. "Boston isn't Stowe, Jack. We are temporary, remember? You can't just come and go on a whim."

"I just thought... maybe we could spend more time together. Explore a new city, build some memories," he countered.

Her frustration broke through, her words more clipped. "Maybe you should've thought of that before running off to NYC on the last day I had here."

"Clara," Jack's voice held a plea, "I'm trying here."

"Just be at the bridge," she snapped.

"I promise," he replied.

After slamming the phone down, Clara paused, her breaths coming fast and uneven, the storm of anger, hurt, and confusion within her threatening to overflow. Her steps toward the cabin were sharp, each one a thud against the ground as if she were trying to stomp away the feelings inside her.

Upon entering, the quiet did not match the chaos in her heart. It was almost as if it were taunting her. Fueled by frustration and the need to do something—anything—she packed with a ferocity that had her clothes being thrown rather than placed into the suitcase. Each garment she handled was a trigger, unleashing flashes of memories with Jack—moments that twisted in her gut, turning sweet recollections bitter.

Something drew her eyes to the journal on the desk. It held so many memories, so many emotions, and she felt the need to pour her feelings into words. Taking a seat, she opened the book, the blank page before her, ready to accept her thoughts.

Two days ago, Jack and I shared an ice cream by the lake. The way the sunlight hit his face, the glint in his eyes as he tried to smear it on my nose... I felt seen, really seen, perhaps for the first time in years.

It's so different from how things were with Ethan. With Ethan, it was like dating a lost boy in a rockstar's body. His dreams, ambitions, and his constant need for attention overshadowed each moment with him. Every date, instead of being a moment between us, felt like another stage for him to perform, another crowd to win over. I often felt more like his manager or caretaker than his girlfriend, constantly picking up after his messes and making sure he was okay.

Yet, there was always a thrill with him. The high of being on his arm as we entered venues, the electric atmosphere of his shows, the late-night jam sessions and impromptu duets. The rush of living on the edge, never knowing what tomorrow might bring. With Ethan, life was a roller coaster—highs and lows. It was intoxicating, the way he'd pull me into his world, where passion and music blended, and every moment felt like a stolen scene.

Deep in her memories, the jarring ringtone shattered her thoughts, pulling her back into the present. Clara's heart fluttered, half-expecting Jack's voice, but the name on the screen froze her momentarily — Ethan. It was if her thoughts had summoned him.

She hesitated before answering. "Hello?"

"Clara? It's me."

His voice sounded disconnected. "Ethan... What do you want?"

"Just wanted to hear your voice," he began with a suggestive lilt. "You know, reminisce a little? Maybe see if you're up for hanging out?"

Clara's brow furrowed. "Isn't that a conversation you should have with your new girlfriend?"

He chuckled, a sound that once held charm, but now grated on her nerves. "She's not you. You know we always had that... spark."

As Ethan's voice droned on, a tidal wave of memories crashed over Clara. The panic when he overdosed, the dread-laden rush to the hospital, opposing against the electrifying sex they shared in the dim glow of their shared bedroom. Each moment, whether painful or intimate, played in her mind like an old film reel.

Clara realized that beneath the trials, there just wasn't an actual connection. Their relationship was an endless cycle of extremes, lacking the stability and depth that actual love brought.

"That 'spark' was just chaos," she told him, her voice cutting through the memories. "We mistook passion for intimacy. And I can't — won't — go back to that chaos."

There was a pause, and for a moment she thought he might argue. But he just sighed. "Had to try, right?"

Clara rolled her eyes. "Goodbye, Ethan."

After ending the call, Clara's pen hovered over her journal once more. This time, the thoughts flowed.

Today I'm hit with this realization—I've always had a thing for the love stories that are a bit... forbidden? Exciting? Definitely more 'ride or die' than 'happily ever after.' It's like how Anne fell hard for Thomas. Their thing was intense, all-consuming, but man, did it crash and burn. And Ethan? His wild unpredictability? Electrifying. But talk about a storm leaving behind its share of chaos. At the time, I was all in, not seeing the damage being done. Now? It's like I'm finding emotional bruises I never knew I had. The more she thought of Anne, the more she felt a kinship. *Anne's passion led her to make a final, irreversible choice in the face of despair. While my story with Ethan didn't have the same consequences, it taught me about decisions and the price of letting passion blind reason.*

And then there's Jack. Is it a story destined to repeat the same mistakes or an opportunity for an alternative path? Clara questioned, feeling histories intertwining with her present.

She sat back, her eyes lingering on the scribbles in her journal. The intertwining stories of Anne and her own life seemed to play out in parallel universes. Her pen was still poised above the paper as she continued to reflect on her own journey with Jack and Ethan.

Then it dawned on her. She remembered overhearing a snippet of conversation in town. Maybe Lila would have the insights she was missing. It felt like a light bulb moment—she realized she should speak with someone who had a relationship with him. Fueled by this thought, she shut her journal and grabbed her keys.

Clara parked outside Lila's shop, taking a moment to gather her courage before stepping out of the car. As she entered, the bell above the door announced her arrival. She found herself surrounded by the timeless elegance of antique dresses, lace gloves, and hats from yesteryears. Lila looked up. Her expression shifted to one of mild surprise upon seeing Clara.

"To what do I owe this unexpected visit?"

Clara hesitated for a moment. "I needed to talk, and I realized there's a lot I don't know. About you, Jack, this town... everything."

Lila's gaze softened, her posture relaxing. "Alright. Sit," she gestured towards a plush couch. "Would you like some tea?"

Clara nodded. As Lila prepared a pot of Earl Grey, Clara took a moment to collect her thoughts. The store, with its charm, felt like a portal to another era, a world where Anne and Thomas might have roamed.

When Lila returned, she poured the steaming liquid into dainty cups. "Speak your mind," she urged.

Taking a sip, Clara began. "I came to Stowe looking for an escape, a story, something... and I found all of that. But I also found Jack. And with him, an entire history, a past, and, honestly, a lot of confusion."

"Jack has that effect," Lila chuckled. "He's a good man, but life hasn't always been kind to him."

Clara paused, gathering her courage. "I'm not blind. I have seen the people in town talking... heard the things that were said."

Lila raised an eyebrow.

"Jack. Us. The stories that keep getting repeated. You're a part of his story, Lila, and I think understanding that could help me navigate mine."

For a moment, there was a heavy silence. "I shouldn't have gone to your place," Lila sighed. "Why dredge up old wounds?"

"But you did, and I see patterns," Clara responded, her voice soft but firm. "And maybe, just maybe, understanding them might prevent history from repeating itself."

Lila hesitated, then gestured towards a seating area, "Alright, but I won't promise you'll like what you hear."

As they took their seats, Clara's hands clasped together, betraying her nervousness. "Why did you hurt him?" she ventured.

Lila's eyes flashed. "Life... love... it's complicated. We were young, impulsive. I made mistakes. Big ones. But Jack wasn't perfect either."

"Everyone has their demons," Clara pressed, searching Lila's face for answers.

"He does," Lila admitted. "Jack used to drink. A lot. It clouded his judgment, made him angry. But it's been years since then. People change, grow. I had my role in our downfall."

Clara pondered on this. "So, why the rumors about him being abusive?"

Lila flinched, guilt clear in her eyes. "I was angry, hurt. I lashed out with words, let people believe things... things that weren't true. But by the time I realized the impact of those rumors, it was too late."

Clara's eyes widened, the implications clear. "So, he never..."

Lila looked away. "He has his flaws, anger among them. But he never raised a hand to me."

The moment hung between them. Clara nodded, grateful for the glimpse of truth, however veiled it was.

Clara hesitated for a moment, feeling vulnerable. "He left for a meeting in NYC," she shared. "Just when I thought we were connecting on a deeper level."

Lila gave a nod, her features softened by a rueful smile. "Jack and his commitment to work. It's always been his shield. When emotions threaten his logic, he often takes the easy way out. Runs, deflects, hides behind responsibilities."

Clara blinked away the sting of tears. "I thought... I thought maybe we could have something more."

Lila sighed. "He likes you, Clara. Quite a bit, I'd bet. But with Jack, sometimes that's a double-edged sword. Caring too much can make him push you away even harder."

Clara managed a weak smile. "I'm leaving tomorrow, anyway."

Lila seemed to take a moment to process this. When she spoke, there was a sense of relief in her voice, mixed with genuine concern. "Probably for the best. For both of you."

Clara nodded, absorbing the bittersweet reality of the moment. "Thanks, Lila."

After their conversation, the women exchanged a meaningful glance—a quiet recognition of the emotions and history they shared. As Clara stepped outside, her walk carried a feeling of closure she hadn't known she was seeking.

When she arrived back at the cabin, she settled down for the evening. Tonight presented a chance to revel in the memories of her time with Jack, to immerse herself in the sweetness of their connection. Yet Clara's pragmatic side whispered reminders of the inevitable march of time. With tomorrow's sunrise, she would press on, leaving behind the charming town and the shadows of a love story that was not to be hers to keep.

She grabbed her bag and moved to the writing nook by the window. Opening her laptop, she dove deep into the world of her novel, a world where Anne and Thomas lived, loved, and suffered. As she immersed herself in their story, it provided an escape from her own confusing reality.

Hours seemed to melt away as she poured her emotions, insights, and newfound clarity into the manuscript. The pain from Ethan, the moments shared with Jack, and the wisdom from her conversation with Lila all found their way into the intricacies of Anne and Thomas's tale.

But as the clock ticked on, the shadows growing longer, she hesitated, leaving the final chapter unwritten. That chapter, she decided, would be penned after reuniting the spirits together, once she was back in Boston, drawing from whatever closure the night might offer her.

As she penned her thoughts, Clara was conscious of the time ticking away. The night promised more than just the hours ahead. It held the anticipation of Jack's return and their shared goal to bring the estranged lovers back together. Midnight was drawing near. With it, not only would Anne and Thomas's love story find its resolution, but so might Clara's own story with Jack.

Before leaving for the bridge, she picked up the locket from the bedside table. The once cold and inanimate object now held warmth and a story — one of love, betrayal, and longing.

As she clutched the locket, an unexpected chill raced down her spine. A fleeting feeling, as if Anne's spirit stood right next to her, urging her on, filled the room. Clara whispered, "We'll find closure tonight, Anne. For both of us."

Drawn by an inexplicable urge, she headed outside. The night sky stretched above her, speckled with countless stars, each one shimmering with its own story, its own secrets. She took a deep, steadying breath, taking in the crisp evening air. In this vast cosmic ballet, where did her own tale fit?

Clara picked out the brightest star, closed her eyes, and breathed out her wish, "I hope for clear skies in this storm of feelings, for the guts to make the choices that need making, and for everything to come together — for Anne, for Thomas, and... for me too."

With her fingers wrapped around the locket, Clara headed toward Willows Bridge.

CHAPTER NINE

A Bridge Between Worlds

Clara approached Willows Bridge, her heart pounding against her ribs. Each beat echoed the fleeting minutes before midnight. The headlights from Ashlyn's car illuminated the gnarled trees lining the road, their twisted limbs casting eerie shadows that tricked her eyes. A full moon hovered low, its shimmering reflections dancing on the water below, yet there was no sign of Jack. The bridge itself rose against the night, its wooden planks slick with dew. Clara could hear the river's gentle murmurs beneath her, its ripples gently kissing the shore. She felt

that if she listened close enough, the night might whisper bac
k.

She took a moment to soak it all in before approaching Ashlyn's car. It was haunting and beautiful, a scene straight out of a gothic novel. She could feel the history all around her. Excitement bubbled within her, but so did fear. Was she meddling in matters beyond her understanding? And then there was the gnawing void—still no Jack.

Clara knocked on the window of Ashlyn's car, her arms wrapped around herself to harness her emotions. She felt vulnerable, as if standing on the cusp of a pivotal chapter in her life—a chapter that risked remaining unwritten. The engine stopped and Ashlyn and stepped out.

She had an almost ethereal quality. Dark hair cascading down, and the fabric of her skirt that caught the light with every gentle sway. The air around them felt alive, vibrating with an energy that was mesmerizing.

When Ashlyn's eyes met Clara's, it was as if they held centuries of wisdom, sorrow, and patience. "I'm glad you're here. Jack?"

"Not yet," Clara swallowed. "I brought the locket. Do you have the ring?"

"Yes," Ashlyn nodded. "You ready?"

Clara's heart raced. "We need to wait for Jack," she asserted.

"We have little time," Ashlyn replied. "It's almost midnight. That is when they were supposed to meet."

"I'm aware," Clara snapped, then softened her voice. "I'm sorry. It's just this is as much Jack's journey as it is ours. He deserves to be here."

There was a beat of silence, the night seeming to hold its breath. Ashlyn answered, "Five minutes. I'll start preparing. Can I have the locket?"

Clara nodded, revealing the intricate piece, its engravings catching the moonlight. "Right here."

"Good." Ashlyn's expression shifted to one of deep concentration. "We'll be working with their energies, amplifying the connection between them. The locket and the ring. They serve as anchors, tethering the spirits of Anne and Thomas to this world. When we unite them, the bond becomes stronger."

As Clara listened, she realized the process was a delicate dance of energy. "How will we... facilitate their reunion?" she asked.

"We'll channel the energy of both artifacts, create a vortex of sorts." Ashlyn replied. "I will lead us in a series of incantations, drawing them closer. Your role is important. You must focus on their love story, envision their union, and urge them to find each other. You will hold the locket, and Jack will hold the ring."

A shiver ran down Clara's spine. She was ready. However, Jack, being late, was a persistent wound. They sat in silence, waiting.

"The window of opportunity is narrowing," Ashlyn warned.

Clara pulled out her phone and dialed Jack's number, the ringing tone echoing her growing impatience. After several rings, his voicemail chimed in. She hesitated for a split second, and then blurted out with a mix of annoyance and sarcasm, "Looks like 'communication' isn't exactly your forte, Jack. I thought our time together merited at least a callback. Or a text. Or even a carrier pigeon, if that's more your speed." After hanging up, she typed a text to accompany her voicemail, trying to keep it light yet pointed. "In case you missed my call–and I'm sure you did–just checking in- C"

She set her phone down and tried to distract herself from the gnawing sensation in her gut. She knew she had planned to move on, but she yearned for closure. A proper goodbye, even if it was over a simple call.

Ashlyn was right. With or without Jack, they had to act. "Let's begin," Clara said, determination seeping into her voice.

The stage was set. Under the vast night sky, two women readied themselves to bridge the divide between two lost souls, hopeful for a reunion that had been centuries in the making.

Willows Bridge became the backdrop to a world where reality and the supernatural danced on the knife-edge of midnight. A chill in the air intensified. The clear night gave way to an eerie mist, wrapping around the bridge like a ghostly shroud.

Ashlyn began, her voice a soft, lilting chant that seemed to meld with the murmurs of the water below and the rustling of the trees. In her hand, a ring sparkled, responding to her cadence, its glow merging with the ambient light that framed her.

Beside her, Clara clutched the locket close to her heart, urging Anne and Thomas towards reconciliation. The memories she had gathered, the stories she had heard, all flooded her mind, shining a hopeful light through the enveloping fog.

As Ashlyn's incantations grew in intensity, the atmosphere rippled. Two ghostly forms coalesced within the mist, their outlines shimmering and uncertain, but present. The translucent figure of Anne looked as if waiting for someone. A few paces away, the specter of Thomas formed, his posture reflecting a life of regret and an eternity of searching.

The air thrummed as Ashlyn's voice reached a crescendo, her words clear and powerful, willing the two spirits closer. Tears streamed down Clara's face as she whispered words of encouragement, guiding the lost lovers towards one another.

The distance between Anne and Thomas shrunk, their forms becoming clearer and more tangible with every passing second. They seemed to recognize each other, their movements hesitant yet filled with hope.

With midnight nearing, the bridge and its surroundings held a collective breath as if expecting a centuries-long awaited reunion.

In the dense mist, Anne and Thomas stood just a few feet apart. Though no words were exchanged, their emotions vibrated through the air — potent and raw.

Anne's form rippled with waves of anger and sadness. Her eyes bore into Thomas with a mix of accusation and pain. The anguish in her form was real, reminding Clara of the countless love stories cut short by societal constraints and misunderstandings. The heavy locket against Clara's chest echoed Anne's heartache. Clara felt her own anger. Ethan's infidelity, Jack's absence. But she had to shove those down deep. Thomas was here and now for Anne, and they could make things right.

Thomas's spirit emanated regret. He extended a hand, shimmering with regret, toward Anne, who initially recoiled.

Their story unfolded in the mist like a move, weaving itself into vivid scenes. These vignettes, strikingly clear, depicted the lovers' encounters — moments brimming with the exhilaration of newfound love, yet overshadowed by the strictures of their time. The laughter and tender touches shared in secret, and the looming shadows of societal condemnation and personal trials that followed. Moments of joy and intimacy — stolen glances at social gatherings, secret meetings under the cover of night, and handwritten letters exchanged in secrecy. But as their love story progressed, the scenes grew darker. Angry confrontations, not with each other, but with families who disapproved, with a society that forbade their union, with a world that couldn't understand the depth of their connection.

Anne's spirit showed her isolation, confined to her room, letters from Thomas being taken away, her pleas going unheard. The society had built walls around her, walls that even her love for Thomas couldn't penetrate.

Thomas's form portrayed his desperation. Efforts to convince her family. The devastating realization that these shackles were too strong to break.

For a moment, the two spirits were once again on the bridge, facing one another. Anne's anger subsided, replaced with an overwhelming sadness. Thomas once again reached out to her. This time, she moved closer, their forms merging, becoming a dance of light and shadow, love and loss.

Their emotions swirled around them, creating past regrets and unspoken words, but in that storm was an undeniable love, a bond that even death and time couldn't sever.

The mist continued to swirl, weaving another memory. Anne, in the solitude of her room, with her hands cradling her swollen belly. She was with child. Her heart, however, was heavy with the secret she carried.

Next, a stolen moment between Anne and Thomas appeared. Under the shelter of an ancient oak tree, they whispered sweet nothings, planning an elopement to escape the constraints of their time. Their love was filled with desperation.

But as the scene shifted, and their reality took its toll. Anne, isolated, her pregnancy becoming more apparent, faced the mounting pressure and judgment of a world that showed no mercy. There was no solace, as Thomas remained unaware of the child they had conceived together.

The next memory was of a lonely Anne in her wedding dress, standing at the edge of the very bridge they were now on, her figure silhouetted by the moon. The secret, and the isolation, proved too much.

As the spirits of Anne and Thomas lingered, their gazes met. In that connection, Thomas realized the child was his, and a profound sadness enveloped him. He hadn't just lost Anne; he had lost a future, a family he never knew existed.

Clara and Ashlyn, witnessing this heart-wrenching revelation, felt the depth of their tragedy and the bittersweetness of their love.

From the enshrouded mists, another scene unfolded. Thomas, held captive in the basement of Anne's family estate. The room was dank, cold, and unwelcoming. The chains around his wrists were as much a symbol of the chains that bound him to his place in the world as they were of the physical restraint imposed upon him.

Through the narrow window, the soft glow of the moon was the only light he could see, reminding him of their countless rendezvous under its gentle gaze. But that night, the moon was a cruel reminder of their missed meeting on the bridge.

Days turned into weeks. The walls of his confinement seemed to close in on him. The only thing that kept him going was the hope of seeing Anne again, of holding her close, of escaping together. But as the days went on, the reality of her absence became all too apparent. Whispers reached his ears, painting a tragic image of Anne's last moments.

Released by their own guilt, Anne's family let Thomas go, but it was too late. The world outside was no longer the same. Everywhere he went, shadows of his lost love followed him, every whisper of the wind sounding like Anne's voice, every shimmer of the moonlit water reminding him of that fateful night.

His heart, once full of love and hope, was now laden with guilt and sorrow. He wandered, searching for solace but finding none. His health deteriorated, and the sparkle in his eyes dimmed. It was clear to all who knew him: Thomas was dying of a broken heart.

In the last scene that the mist presented, Thomas was seen on the very bridge where he and Anne were to meet. He looked out at the horizon, perhaps searching for a sign of his love, a hope that had long evaded him. And as the first light of dawn broke, he took one last breath, his heart giving out, hoping to reunite with his love in the realm of spirits.

But it was not to be. In her anger, Anne could not see him there waiting all those years, right by her side. A transformation occurred within Anne's spirit. The realization that Thomas, too, had suffered, that he had remained tethered to her side through the veils of time and sorrow, dissolved her anger. His unwavering presence, invisible to her eyes but now undeniable, bridged the chasm of misunderstanding that had kept them apart.

In a moment of forgiveness, the specters of Anne and Thomas closed the gap. As they touched, a luminous energy enveloped them, and their forms merged. The surrounding light grew, pulsating with the power of their united spirits.

Clara and Ashlyn watched as Anne and Thomas, now a radiant entity braided together with a third strand, ascended toward a brighter realm. Their love, tested by time and tragedy, had not only endured, but had become the key to their transcendence.

In this ultimate act of union and forgiveness, they left behind the chains of earthly sorrow, moving into a place where love knows no bounds. Clara stood still, her emotions a mess. Willows bridge, though silent now, had seen countless stories unfold. It had borne witness to promises made and hearts broken. Tonight, it had seen two souls unite, but also witnessed Clara's heartbreak.

She stared into the distance, searching for a familiar silhouette, longing for Jack's presence. But all she saw was an empty path illuminated by the moon. Every tick of the clock was a sharp reminder of Jack's absence. His promise, their plans, the future they might have had - they all felt like distant memories now.

With a heavy sigh, Clara reflected on Anne and Thomas. Though separated by tragedy and time, had found their way back to each other. Their love story had crossed the barriers of life and death. But hers was a different story. One where love was a fleeting moment, a beautiful dream that disappeared with the morning light.

"I wanted to believe in us, Jack," she whispered, her voice almost lost in the wind.

She approached Ashlyn, who was still absorbing the surrounding energies. "Thank you," Clara began. "For everything. And, as always, send me the bill for our consult."

Ashlyn looked up, her sharp eyes softening. "Clara, I did this for Anne, not as a business transaction."

Clara smiled. "You can't always work for free. And besides," she glanced back at the bridge, the last traces of Anne and Thomas's spirits fading, "you have a unique gift. Perhaps you should consider a new venture—reuniting lost souls."

Ashlyn chuckled, the mood lightening a bit. "That has a nice ring to it, doesn't it?"

They both stood there for a moment, letting the night sink in. Ashlyn, sensing Clara's sadness, placed a comforting hand on her shoulder. "Every love story is different, Clara. Remember, sometimes the journey itself holds more beauty than the destination."

Clara nodded. "I know, and even if Jack isn't part of my final chapter, I'm grateful for the pages he filled."

With a final shared glance, the two women parted ways. Clara, while heartbroken, pushed forward. □
The fire Jack had ignited within her—passion and a longing to love and be loved—would continue to guide her toward whatever adventures lay ahead.

She couldn't sleep that night, the silence in the house too pronounced. Accustomed to sharing the space with Anne's spirit, its absence was felt. Instead, she found solace in writing in her journal, capturing her thoughts until the first light of dawn graced the sky.

As sunlight brushed the horizon with hues of gold and pink, Clara finished packing her belongings, each item stirring memories of her time spent in Stowe. The aroma of her morning coffee blended with the musty scent of old wood, evoking a surge of unexpected emotions. The rented cabin had been a place of solace, creativity, and surprisingly love.

After closing her suitcase, she paused, eyes sweeping over the rental one last time. With her car packed, she drove toward the bridge. She took a moment to park and stepped out to a scene wrapped in magic. The gentle shimmer of the water below mirrored the dawn sky. She could almost imagine Thomas and Anne looking down at her.

Memories of Jack—of their first awkward meeting and the connection that blossomed—flooded her thoughts. It was ironic how this bridge, marking the beginning of their journey, now framed its end. With a bittersweet smile, Clara whispered into the breeze, hoping her words would find Jack, "Thank you for being a chapter in my story." Then she returned to her car, ready to follow the day and embrace the unknown.

The car's steady hum was her sole companion. The road ahead beckoned her towards Boston and the uncharted beyond, each mile a step from who she had been to who she was becoming.

She switched on the radio and a melody filled the air, capturing the moment—a song of heartbreak and starting over. Everything happens for a reason. It seemed the universe itself was affirming her belief in new beginnings.

A smile crept across Clara's face, her eyes glistening with tears not of sadness, but of recognition. Changed, evolved, and enriched by her experiences and the taste of fleeting love, she drove on. The promise of tomorrow called, and she was eager to answer.

CHAPTER TEN

Second Chances

Clara approached Boston, watching as the city's skyline cut a familiar silhouette against the sky. It was a change from Stowe's quiet nature. Gone were the soothing whispers of wind through the trees, now replaced by the urban symphony of honking cars and loud pedestrians. Starlit nights gave way to ever-lit evenings, constant city lights harsh compared to the peaceful skies she had grown accustomed to. Yet, for all its hustle and noise, Boston was home.

She navigated through the streets, readjusting to the angry drivers and finding her parking spot that cost almost as much as her rent. A piece of her heart had stayed in Vermont, with its quiet nights and the stories that seemed to flow like the river under that old bridge—especially those involving Jack. When she approached her building. A wave of nostalgia hit her. She made her way to her apartment, the keys heavier than she remembered. With a click, she unlocked the door and stepped into a realm of memories. The air smelled of the past — a mix of her favorite vanilla candles, the slight musk of old books, and the ghost of Ethan's aftershave.

This space, once brimming with shared dreams, now seemed too vast, its empty corners amplifying the quiet of her solitude. Yet, as she returned her belongings to their familiar spots, a sense of empowerment emerged.

The buzz of her phone snapped her out of her reverie. An incoming text displayed his name—her heart raced, but not with excitement, rather a pang of anxiety. The message read, "Saw you were home. Can we *talk*? I miss you."

Clara stared at the screen, memories of their last intense "talks", the undertones that overshadowed actual communication, and that they were on different paths, all resurfacing. A previous version of herself might've been lured into replying, but this was a new Clara. She had communed with spirits, unearthed age-old tales of love, and discovered the depths of her inner strength and tenacity.

Who needs Ethan or even Jack? The lightness of the thought was grounding, reminding her of her independence and the joys of self-reliance. Life was too short to be tied to anyone's games or whims, and Clara was ready to embrace every facet of her newfound freedom.

She swiped the notification away, choosing to leave the message unanswered. This was her story now, and she was determined to write it on her own terms.

Unfortunately, her determination wasn't as infallible as she had hoped. In the days that followed, navigating her apartment felt like she was the lead in a tragicomedy tailored to her life. Every corner, every shadow, seemed to dance with memories of Ethan. From the mismatched socks he left behind like a trail to those post-it notes scribbled with what appeared to be an alien script, decipherable to no one but him. She found herself on the verge of calling him more times than she cared to admit.

But the pièce de résistance was a bottle of tequila. Not just any tequila, but the one they'd used for 'make-up margaritas' after their many spats. It was their silly tradition: arguing, then reconciling over salt-rimmed glasses and regrettable decisions.

With the bottle in her hand, Clara entertained the idea of a solo margarita night. After all, tequila had a magical way of blurring reality, right? But then, a smirk forming on her lips, she had a better idea. Marching to the sink, she unscrewed the cap and poured it out.

"So long, liquid bad decisions," she chuckled, watching as the amber liquid swirled down the drain. This act wasn't about discarding memories, but asserting control. Her heart might still be on the mend, but Clara was calling the shots now. Well, not those kinds of shots, anyway.

The next day Clara sat down at her writing desk, pushing aside the remnants of her old life. The familiar feel of her keyboard beneath her fingers acted as an anchor, grounding her to her passion. As she pulled up her manuscript, images of the bridge, of Anne's form, and Thomas's lingering presence, filled her mind, as vivid as if she'd just experienced them.

Each word she typed was tinged with the past - the love she'd witnessed, the heartbreak, and the resolution she had helped bring about. There were moments of hesitation where she'd lean back and rub her temples, trying to find the right words. There were tears as memories, both beautiful and painful, made their way onto the pages. But there was also a profound sense of catharsis. Every sentence, every paragraph brought her closer to closure, not just for Anne and Thomas, but for herself as well.

Once the final chapter was complete, a sense of accomplishment washed over her. But one piece remained: the title. She wanted something that encapsulated the heart of the story, the love, the loss, and the undeniable power of Willows Bridge. After a few moments of contemplation, the perfect title came to her: "Bridging the Heart."

With a deep breath, Clara packaged the manuscript and sent it off to her publisher. The emotions she felt were dizzying - excitement at sharing her story with the world, apprehension about its reception, but above all, hope. Hope that her tale of enduring love would resonate with readers everywhere.

A few days later, there was an unexpected knock on Clara's door. She sighed, knowing that distinctive rhythm. Ethan always had a way of announcing his presence, even before she saw his face. After taking a moment to compose herself, Clara approached the door, rehearsing her boundaries.

"Ethan, I'm not letting you in," she called out, her hand on the door but not opening it.

"Clara, come on. We need to talk," came the pleading voice from the other side.

She closed her eyes, drawing in a deep breath. "We've talked enough, Ethan. It's over."

Silence reigned for a moment, broken only by a defeated sigh from the other side. Clara leaned her forehead against the door for a moment, willing herself not to open it.

She was just settling back with a book when another knock echoed in her apartment. Her irritation spiked. "Seriously, Ethan? I told you—" This time she flung open the door, ready to confront him, but stopped mid-sentence. It wasn't Ethan standing there.

The hallway seemed to stretch on forever between them. Clara, with a face etched in disbelief, eyed Jack. Her guard was up, emotions teetering between surprise and skepticism.

Jack looked worn. His eyes were a shade darker, maybe from sleepless nights or perhaps from regrets. He hesitated, then stepped forward, stopping when he sensed her need for distance. "Can we... talk?"

She eyed him for a moment longer before nodding and stepping aside. The door opened wider, but the emotional barrier remained. Once inside, Jack paused. The walls of the apartment bearing witness to another fragile moment between two souls.

"I know I owe you an explanation," he began, his voice hoarse. "And I'm hoping you'll hear me out."

She nodded again, folding her arms. "Start talking."

Jack rubbed the back of his neck, a gesture Clara recognized as his tell when he was nervous. "I should've been upfront with you. The trip to NYC? It wasn't for work. I was in Boston."

Her brow furrowed. "Boston? Why?"

He hesitated, the raw vulnerability clear in his gaze. "For us. Or at least the possibility of us. You see, I had an interview. I wanted to be closer, to see if... if there was a chance for something between us. But I didn't want to tell you right away. I didn't want you to feel trapped or obligated."

Clara's eyes flashed. "Why didn't you show up at the bridge, Jack? Why didn't you answer your phone?"

Jack looked down, struggling to find the right words. "I wanted to. God, Clara, more than you'll ever know."

She blinked, trying to process the revelation. "Then why didn't you?"

His eyes looked haunted when he locked them with her. "You know, everything changed on my way back from that interview, just a few miles outside of Boston. All it took was a moment. A truck swerved into my lane, and suddenly... I was caught in this pitch-black world. All I could hear was metal twisting and glass breaking." She looked more closely at him. He *did* look like he had been hit by a truck.

"Why didn't you reach out when you could? You have my number. It's been over a month!"

"I was in an induced coma for a week." His voice wavered. "When I woke up, I felt lost. I thought I'd ruined everything with you. That I'd lost any chance of being a part of your life."

He took a shaky breath, and continued, "When the job offer from Boston came in, it felt like the universe was offering me a way back. A sign that maybe, just maybe, I could make things right. Even if it meant laying my heart bare and risking rejection. I looked up your address and here I am."

She stared at him, and her heart raced, conflicting emotions waging a war within. She felt betrayed, the raw pain of the nights she spent wondering why he'd abandoned her at the bridge still fresh. But hearing about the accident, seeing the remorse in Jack's eyes, and the physical scars that marred his skin evoked a deep sympathy. And intertwined with all these feelings was that undeniable thread of hope that had always connected them.

Jack stepped forward. "Clara," he began, his voice thick with emotion, "I'm not here to offer excuses. I made decisions, and they had consequences. All I can offer you now is the truth. The truth about the accident, about the job, about how much I missed you, and how much I regretted not being able to tell you everything sooner."

She watched him, taking a moment to absorb his words, letting them sink in. The memories of their time together, the laughs, the shared moments, the chemistry, all came flooding back. But she also remembered the nights of doubt, the uncertainty that had clouded their relationship.

Jack's eyes lit up with hope, but he tempered it with caution, "Clara, things are going to be different. We can take it slow, get to know each other again. No pressures, no expectations." He paused. "No strings attached. I'll do anything you need."

She smirked, that playful glint in her eyes returning. "There is one thing you can do right now," she said. With that, she walked towards her kitchen, rummaged through a drawer, and returned holding a pair of bright pink rubber gloves.

"Time for you to become the dishwashing superhero you were always meant to be. First task: conquer Mount Dirty-dishes!" Her attempt at a stern look dissolved into giggles.

Jack blinked, taken aback for a split second, but then his own grin matched hers in mischief. "Well, let me see if I can be of any help."

"Where are you staying at?" Clara asked.

Elbow-deep in suds, Jack shot her a glance. "I'm in corporate housing while I hunt for a place. It's a bit like living in a fancy hotel, minus the room service. How's that for glamour?"

Clara handed him another dish, a smirk playing on her lips. "Oh, the luxury! So, you're basically on a prolonged vacation with chores?"

"Exactly," Jack chuckled, splashing water her way. "But without the beach and the Piña coladas. I'm living the dream, one lease application at a time."

"Sounds delightful," Clara laughed, dodging the water. "Need a local guide to navigate the treacherous waters of Boston real estate?"

"I might take you up on that," he said, placing a clean plate on the rack. "But only if you promise not to make me wear these pink gloves outside of dish duty."

"No promises," she quipped, and they both burst into laughter, the tension and distance of the past melting away.

"On a serious note," he began, his tone shifting, "can I take you out? A proper date? Just you and me, rediscover each other."

Clara nodded with a smile. "I'd like that."

Jack leaned over, placing a gentle kiss on her forehead. He sat up, making moves to get dressed. "I should head home, give you some space."

But as he headed to the door, Clara reached out, her fingers wrapping around his wrist. "Stay for a bit," she said.

Jack's eyes softened, transporting them back to Willows Bridge. The worn-out wood, the creaking sounds in the wind, the memories it cradled. It was a bridge that had witnessed countless sunrises and sunsets, alongside many stories of love and loss.

"Remember that day when we first bumped into each other?" Jack said. "The sunshine, the cool breeze... and us, caught up in the middle of it all. I knew then that I had stumbled into something extraordinary."

Clara nodded, a single tear rolling down her cheek, yet her smile remained firm. "I do. Willows Bridge... Annes Bridge..."

She leaned into him, closing her eyes. "Love is a lot like that bridge. It endures wear and tear, faces the harsh elements, but it stands strong, connecting one side to the other."

He wrapped his arms around her, their heartbeats synchronizing. "So, what do we do now?" Jack asked.

Looking up at him, Clara's eyes were hopeful. "We cross the bridge and move forward. Every story is unique, and ours is just beginning."

Outside, the city lights danced, casting the buildings into striking silhouettes against the evening sky. Far away in Vermont, the Willows Bridge remained steadfast, a sym-

bol of their love, and heralding a fresh start for Clara and J
ack.

Chapter Eleven

Afterword

When you grow up in New England, ghost stories are a part of life. They're told around campfires, during sleepovers, and on dark, snowy evenings. One story that always intrigued me was that of Emily's Bridge in Stowe, Vermont. Some say it's true, others just a tale made up to keep kids from jumping off the bridge. To me, as a fiction writer, the line between fact and fable isn't as important. What matters is the story's power to captivate, to chill, and to charm.

Writing "Bridging the Heart"and the entire "Kindred Spirit Mysteries" series has been like a journey back to my roots. It's funny how weaving these tales feels a bit like coming home. I get to walk the paths I did as a kid, and remember the thrill of thinking that maybe, just maybe, the shadows held something more.

Through these stories I've tried to create a little world where the spirits of New England might not just be real, but also have something to say. It's not about proving ghosts exist. It's about tapping into that sense of wonder and possibility that makes life a bit more interesting.

Even though I can't bring spirits together, I like to think that by sharing these stories, I'm putting something good into the world. Maybe these tales can be a bridge of their own—a way for readers to connect with the past, with each other, and with the places that I've loved all my life.

Thank you for joining me on this adventure. Every story is a piece of me, and I hope you find something in them that resonates with you, too.

About the Author

Beth Connor is a weaver of tales, captivated by writing and fueled by a love for storytelling.

Beth's creative pursuits are a reflection of her life philosophy, and she is always searching for new ways to expand her knowledge and understanding of the world. She has a keen eye for detail and a remarkable ability to create vivid, dynamic settings that resonate with her audience.

Beth's talent has earned her recognition as the author of several published works, including the captivating novels "Hollow City" and The Isdralan Chronicles Series as well as a contributor to many anthologies. Beth is also an accomplished audiobook narrator and the host of the popular podcast, "Crossroads Cantina."

Despite her many endeavors, Beth remains down-to-earth and dedicated to living authentically, true to her passions and values. She resides in the Pacific Northwest with her husband, two children, and canine companions, who bring her boundless inspiration and delight.

Also by

ALSO BY BETH CONNOR:

Hollow City

The Isdralan Chronicles:
Micah and the Candles of Time
Prodigy of Flame
Bridge of Blood and Thornes

Kindred Spirit Mysteries:
The Secret of Misthaven Island
Bridging the Heart